Praise for DARK FA

"Koja crafts the future that the ravers of the 1990[...] immersive and propulsive cyberpunk outing. . . . [...] prose, Koja captures minds that see a thousand worlds at once, lives live[...] 150 beats per minute, and the complicated, messy reality that lies beneath the endless search for the perfect night out. This is sure to delight fans of Jeff Noon and mind-bending speculative fiction."
PUBLISHERS WEEKLY

"Visionary. Stunning. A near-future vision of clubbing culture that takes us beyond virtual reality but, at the same time, presents an intimate look at the life of artists. Koja proves once again that she is a master of her craft."
ALMA KATSU, author of *The Fervor* and *The Deep*

"You don't read *Dark Factory* so much as slam dance your way through its glittering labyrinth of art, tech, danger, and lust. Meticulously envisioned and impeccably performed, this book lives and breathes far beyond its pages, providing an experience more akin to experimental theater than traditional literature; once again, Koja drags fiction kicking and screaming into the future, where it belongs."
MARYSE MEIJER, author of *The Seventh Mansion* and *Heartbreaker*

"Some writers are born to spin tales from the shadows. Kathe Koja is one such author. *Dark Factory* is a unique and esoteric experience. A journey into the throbbing heart of creativity itself. Where we find kisses and cuts. A fantastic story."
S.A. COSBY, NYT bestselling author of *Razorblade Tears* and *Blacktop Wasteland*

"Koja's books demand your attention. Her dense, poetic prose and deftly turned details require close reading. But Koja's books also reward your attention. Reading a Koja novel is always a profound experience: disorienting and inspiring by turns."
CORY DOCTOROW, NYT bestselling author of *Little Brother* and *Homeland*

"Whether you party or work in XR, *Dark Factory* is an absolute must to pick up. *Ready Player One* was what the industry originally looked to for inspiration for building virtual platforms, but *Dark Factory* is a closer look at how things actually are."
K. GUILLORY, THE METACULTURE

tastes, choices, wit, and unparalleled skill. In a career brimming with immersive fiction, here, now, a novel about immersion itself. Nobody could've told this story but Kathe Koja. Dark Factory is written with the appetite and buzzing of a debut novel, but the sureness of a modern master. Each sentence takes a stand, makes a joke, reveals a truth, so that halfway deep, the reader is wholly and truly immersed."
JOSH MALERMAN, NYT bestselling author of *Bird Box* and *Daphne*

"*Dark Factory* reminds us that Kathe Koja is not only a great writer, but an important one. Bolstered by inventive audiovisual supplements, the book is both intimate and epic, an ensemble genre-bender that envisions new possibilities for the novel as narrative form. This is a daring work of multisensory and multimedia immersion, an exemplar of Koja's career-long commitment to dissolving boundaries—between genres and delivery systems, between body and mind, between story and reader, between virtual and real. This is a propulsive, wickedly funny literary party; enter the Factory, lose yourself, and dance."
MIKE THORN, author of *Shelter for the Damned*, *Darkest Hours*, and *Peel Back and See*

"As onetime gatekeeper to some of New York's most legendary nightclubs, I can assure you there has never been one quite like Dark Factory. Situated in an imminent, perhaps even parallel time, this is a club Philip K. Dick might have envisioned, designed to provide the ultimate heightened user experience. Here virtual and altered reality mix and combust to create a new kind of collective Dionysian ecstasy, sensually intoxicating and potentially transgressive. Behind this Dark Factory, Ari Regon is the creative alchemist looking to push boundaries of what a club experience, if not life itself might be. Meta-author Kathe Koja builds a hyperdetailed, tangibly peopled, noirish world around Ari's own world-building mission with all its challenges, foibles, and loves. But this world doesn't stop there; it continues with you, because Dark Factory isn't merely a book; it's an ongoing interactive 'club' experience that you may, indeed are encouraged to enter, revel in, expand and transmutate with. It's an explosively unpredictable scene, so if you're adventurous, limitlessly curious, and a bit crazy put on your 'tiara' and enter *Dark Factory* at your own risk and delight—you're on the list."
JORGE SOCARRAS, singer and writer, and former staffer at New York's Danceteria, Area, Palladium, Tunnel, MK and Big Haus

DARK FACTORY

KATHE KOJA

Meerkat Press
Asheville

ISBN-13 978-1-946154-87-3 (Paperback)
ISBN-13 978-1-946154-88-0 (Ebook)

Author Photo by Rick Lieder
Cover design by Tricia Reeks
Book design by Tricia Reeks

Stock photos and composite imagery from AdobeStock.com and Pexels.com

Printed in the United States of America

Published in the United States of America by
Meerkat Press, LLC, Asheville, NC
www.meerkatpress.com

The Dark Factory project combines Kathe Koja's writing and her immersive event creation for an ongoing fiction experience unlike any other.

DARK PARK is the encore to DARK FACTORY: the morning after the night at the club.

You can catch up with the story online, via Instagram and Twitter and Facebook, or by contacting the team directly at DarkFactory.club

If you're reading this, you're already part of the experience.

DarkFactory.club

MINOS DOC title TK production notes/personal

Whatever happens, this one's on Fux.

***

I wasn't working on anything—round 2 Greenlite grant to apply
for, supposed to put together a proposal, I just wasn't seeing
any of it. Then Meghan Sorin contacts me to shoot a studio
launch event, not remotely my type of gig, and the date's
already booked for Drag Rodeo, not my type of gig either but
Santi is a friend. So I turn her down. But I couldn't get a
jitney flight to Lisbon, wind storms, Santi had to cancel. And
Fux was at the Sorin launch, they went over with Upsetta and
her crew, Fux starts sending me starred clips, Serge Serge
Serge look look.

Visuals are fucking stunning. Like Bosch, Caravaggio—primeval
trees, rusted-out machine carcasses, fireworks, fire, people
trancing, people crawling around in the weeds, the DJ's up
on a platform like a statue, or a tableau vivant, I'm grabbing
everything, grabbing and logging. Then it starts blowing up,
people posting all type of shit, a lot of transcendental woo shit
that I cannot get with. But I can't get away from those visuals.

So I message Sorin. No response. 2 weeks, 4 weeks, finally

she responds back but she says her DJ's not down anymore, he doesn't want to be followed around by a crew. I say, What if I shot solo with a Piccolo rig, fly on the wall, and leave the first time he asks me to? No response again, but it felt like something might be happening. Then she says, Short notice, but could you do a meeting today?

I say, DJ changed his mind?

She says, Ari wants to meet you.

***

Out from the lav in a whiff of sweetish smoke, a few fortifying Kuba Kuba puffs, Ari pauses for Sergey the filmmaker—black braids and red wristband, red camera rigging looped like veins across his sky blue t-shirt—Sergey nimble, backward as Felix advances, head high, gaze fully inward, down the hallway lined with event posters, *RIDE THE LIGHT, BANG & BLOOM XIII,* a brand-new *QUEST FEST* with Felix's own stylized face gazing back. Meghan follows, blue leather shirtdress, intent on her phone—"Then it is available? We can get on-site?"—as they all turn the corner toward the glassy studio space, the Mix Masters hosts waiting, music already thumping, "Balcony" of course.

And Ari feels Felix sigh, Felix beside him so beautiful and tired, no time today even to shave so "One second," he says, hand up to halt Sergey's camera, halt Meghan too to give them space, their own space and "You want to go back to the hotel?" his murmur, "after this? We'll talk to these people, me and Meg will talk. Then you and me are out."

"Out till tonight?"

"Out till tonight," a nod, a promise: tonight will be long and loud and crowded like all their nights are now, but the hotel is small and very private, an old stone convent with slit windows, and a vertical plunge pool adjacent to their suite, the concierge said it was once used for baptisms; Felix was in it last night, upright floating, eyes closed in the cold green water . . . Felix is clearly over the promo and interviews, the remixes of the 12-inch, the run-up to Quest Fest, Felix only wants to work on a new performance he calls his lab, working so hard that he needs to be nudged to stop, to breathe, drink some wine, kiss and fuck and rest and dream.

But Felix is even more attentive to him, even more watchful, ever since Dark Park: Felix very silent at that morning-after afternoon table, until Ari spilled coffee with his clumsy swollen hand, sprained hand, blue bruised chin and *Where were you?* Felix stern to Ilias, righting that cup. *Where was Gus, where was fucking anybody—*

Gussie was right there! Ilias defensive, wired, swamped by turmoil and sudden success, *Ari was all right! Right, Ari?* and his own nod, it was no one's fault, no fault at all, one minute he was dancing and the next all he could see was flesh and the dirt, mobbed to the ground until Gus elbowed and dragged him upright again. Then the fire lit the sky like God's own spotlight, Ilias said the trees were so old no fireworks could hurt them, Ilias said *Nobody got hurt! I told the fucking mayor—*

But Felix had turned away from Ilias, turned back to him and *From now on,* Felix said, very firm, *you stay where I am.*

Today he and Felix are here, tomorrow they will be somewhere else, together at the center of whatever this is, this living speeding branching apparatus, everybody who comes at them wants something—validation, an explanation, an interview, a linki, a job, a fuck, Uni's team screens them but they still get through: the dancers, the fans, the Y producers and festival bookers, a DJ whose handle is Fuxury pushing hard to do a b2b, a *neue Klänge* collective in Munich, a queer lifestyle app called Aussi, *You're our perfect brandbassadors!*—all in that hot vacuum of celebrity, shoutouts and callouts on Beat Buzzer and Afterglow and Pyramid, so many that sometimes he just stares at it all, Uni set up a spillover MePage for him and he stares at that too; and at the journos too, not only industry but news sites, KZN and News Immediate and NYNY, even some political journos, Uni says *There's a lot of people out there looking to score points, nothing to turn blue over but we want to be careful . . .* And all of it multiplying on its own, faster and faster, what is that called? exponential? starting things, ending things, changing things, changing people—Meghan has changed, Meg dancing in that fire with Suze of all people, and *I understand, now,* her hand on his arm outside the Indigo guest room, as wired as Ilias but blissful, she still smelled like the scorched trees. *What Suze calls the Artemis wilderness—*

The what?

—and I've just messaged Clara, I won't be working on the game anymore. AWIP is meant for you, to give you all the tools you need.

What tools, but it was not a question: Meg, and Ilias and Gussie, the jittery mayor and overwhelmed Polícia, Border Security red-flagging his name, they all expect him to have answers, they all seem to credit him with, or suspect him of, a level of control that is almost funny, it is funny, Ari Superman—Because the one thing he knows for sure is that everything comes from that spin, and everything is spinning so much faster now, is so much bigger than he ever could have dreamed, demanding just as much as it gives, *an entire level of presence,* Max wrote about that in his notes, Max on that X'd-out beach, has Max changed too—

—but now Felix is smiling again, smiling at him, Felix his love, his star, what is it called, the star that points the way home? and "Maybe grab some food?" Felix says. "That taverna, with the jackfruit kebabs—"

"And some wine," his own smile, and when he smiles everyone smiles, Meg, the studio hosts, Sergey's camera lights up again and "Meg," he says, turning with Felix toward the studio doors. "Come on and talk."

"Oh, no, they only need you two—Look," showing her phone, "I finally heard from the site manager, that monsignor—"

"Come on," still smiling, a different smile, authority, he is learning how and when to use that too. And she nods, and Felix takes the chair nearest the door while a third chair is hastily positioned, as "Cool outfit," says one of the hosts, while a tech clips a lav mic to her mottled blue lapel.

"It's from Desplanets," she says. "Mushroom leather."

"Mycelium," Ari says to no one, to the air, as the music segues from "Balcony" to the show intro, as Sergey crouches in the rootlike twist of cables, watching with one bright augmented eye.

MINOS DOC title TK production notes/personal

Meeting was in the Birds of Paradise gamescape, that super-constructed patina, fine for games but for pure visuals, no grain, no thanks. Took a minute to get the login to work, and Regon's already there, this blue streak thing, like Let's do this. Some other beta players too, but no one besides me could see him, and because I'm with him they can't see me either. Privacy feature? He says, Power user, and laughs, but not at me. I say, You play a lot? and he says, I never come in here except for work.

So I take the hint and tell him I want to shoot whatever they've got going on next, my dime not his. Regon's a friendly dude but it's clear he's in charge, so I'm prepped for questions, but what he asks is, Why did you pick that avatar? and I don't have an answer, this duck-looking thing, the eyes just looked like lenses to me. Then he says, Why's your production company called Tutto Bene? And I say—no idea why, it just came out—Why is Perez called Mister Minos?

He likes that, he says, All right, I'll talk to Felix, we'll make it work. Then he's done, disappeared, and immediately I'm visible, because some avatar with bigass wings and a head like a paint bucket flaps up and asks have I seen Max. Tf is Max.

Meghan Sorin sends on the agreement, very tight, rights, access, process, who's my imaging tech, who's my audio tech, who's doing post. We finally got it signed, put together a shooting schedule, and I say, Thanks a lot, you know, for wanting to book me in the first place. But she says, Actually it was Ari's idea, he saw one of your films and said you'd be perfect for Dark Park.

TF?! Why didn't he tell me that? Sorin doesn't know which film, is it *Housefly*? No way it's *Constructive Panic*. *Housefly* won at Atlanta Docs, at Jugband, Creative Imaging award, it has to be *Housefly*.

I can't even look at those things anymore, but which one?

***

The light filters through the fronds of the Phoenician palms, perpetual light as calm and unchanging as this sun, a limbo light—or limbic, Davide's favorite, the paleomammalian cortex response, Davide used to call it the *oh fuck* button—as Max shifts back against the trunk no longer scarred with X's, Max writing in the air, ending with THIS IS THE LUX PERPETUA. Some people call what he writes "Maxisms," like aphorisms, or koans, but all of it is really a story, the real story of all of this.

Marfa calls those people his birds, those beta players, students and devs and Y artists who came to the game through Mathias's Dark Park gateway, and who now, in various states of dazed belief and dazzled need, come to find him, thank him, tell him what being in B of P means to them, ask what it means to him, and collect the Maxisms as encouragement, the kind of benediction he would once have wanted for himself but never could have asked for, too frozen by unhappiness, by misplaced pride. Once Adam Kaiser came, but did not seek him out, *people need a way to be lost,* is Adam still lost, is Adam still at Kunstfarm? *If everything partakes of reality,* do you still need a teacher to teach you that? Maybe Adam needs a teacher now.

Davide has started to appear in here again, furtive, seemingly unblockable though *Who cares,* Clara's curt shrug, *he can't access anything anymore, let him see what he's missing.* Clara is still hurt by Davide's betrayal, what she thinks of as betrayal, though Davide thinks *he* was betrayed, by Clara and by Mathias, even by Max, for reasons Max does not understand but suspects has to do with those birds, who all seem to believe that what happened on the beach happened because of Max's agency . . . Mathias calls it *Floatsam Beach, like "flotsam" but it floats!* Mathias still the basic explorer avatar with a mouthful of green fangs, Mathias whose company acquired B of P along with Fantastic Fantoms the way a tidal wave acquires the shore: now Mathias's vastly funded crew edits that environment, retools their tools, fixes bugs, and pushes through to plateaus of completion what can never truly be complete; Mathias, Max knows, understands that distinction.

And he understands Mathias much better than he used to, Mathias who still treats him with that same joking bro bonhomie, sharing ideas and philosophies, sharing news—*B of P's wishlisting top three on Wowzr, Gamer Garfman tagged us as a Play or Die, Leon Cardenal plans to haul the whole TECMA board in here*—and inviting him to some new dev conference *In the Hideaway, you know the Hideaway? Insomnious is hosting, Tom and Jason, Click and Drag,* the Insomnious logo popping into the air above the surfline like an absurd add-on moon, its slick rotating nimbus advertising **Transmedial Identities • Massively Scaled Synchronicities • We Never Sleep.** But when he shook his head to all of it, Mathias said he understood: *No stress, Canary, you don't have to leave your habitat. I wanted Minos to come too and talk about Minosland, but he's all balls-deep in this Quest Fest crap*—Quest Fest, whose quest is that? And what is Minosland?

Meghan Sorin would know, but Meghan has left the game entirely—Clara saddened by that departure too, though not surprised; Marfa told him that, Marfa showed him the videos, *Sorin got totally Dark Parked, cashed all her Fantom shares, and now she wheels fulltime for Ari and Felix*—Meghan the only one of them who traveled on-site for that mystic show under those strange trees, Meghan dancing, Felix muddy and sublime, and Ari radiant beyond radiance, no wonder they swarmed him, no wonder he fell.

He misses Ari.

Not in the old way, the physical walk-and-smoke way, he needs so little physical presence now that even the time he spends eating and sleeping and talking with Marfa is enough, more than enough; he knows Marfa thinks that the physical world is too demanding for him, feels too "real," but she has it exactly backward: that world is not too concrete, but too incomplete, it still supports, feeds, so many questions, questions that in here have been answered, in here is a complexity that approaches absolute simplicity. When he sits on the bottom of this ocean for hours and days that are not hours or days but only one continuous moment, that outside world still built around chronos time, or xronos as Davide used to spell it, feels both hysterically busy and disjointedly lost, and is no place he wants to be.

But he misses Ari. And Ari never comes into the game, or if he does—as he recently did, Mathias said *I saw your pal dropped in for a nanochat with some duck*—he comes in shield mode, to do whatever he needs to do, then leave. Ari is still part of xronos time, but no longer fully bound by it either, the way a cloud's shadow rides the ground while the cloud itself floats thirty thousand feet above, how much of that does Ari understand? He and Ari need to talk—

—but now something small is tickling his jaw, a little wriggling iridescence, a bug that unfurls into a tiny banner: MARFACARP, Marfa is calling him. There are easier ways, but her preferred means of getting his attention is via message bug, *It's not a bug, it's a feature! See, I can make game jokes too.* Right now Marfa is working at the dusty little table in his stuffy little room—he can feel her there, he can almost always feel when she is there—busy with her interviews, the last one was with *One of those Fear of God witchburners, now I need one of your birds for balance. Which one?*

I don't know. I don't know any of them.

Well, you should, they know all about you, what games you played, where you went to school. They look up to you—

I never asked them to.

Fine. I'll find one to talk to, I always find people to talk to.

What about Ari, you talk to him?

Ari still won't talk to me.

He feels around in the grass, sifting through bent blades and tiny pebbles and twists of concertina wire until he finds the bug, closes his hand around it then sighs and closes his eyes, feeling the atmosphere around him change, contract, feeling the tiara around his head, the headache, it seems like he always has a headache and "Max," Marfa says, Marfa all vitality in a yellow sweatshirt that says HIVE MIND, she smells like fresh coffee and tea tree oil. "Let's go, it's a gorgeous—Max, hey, you OK?"

"I'm fine . . . You moved that?" pointing to the mask, Felix's horned and eyeless mask sitting now on the end of the little table desk, not balanced anymore on the boxes in the corner.

Already at the door she turns, looks, frowns, shrugs. "I didn't. You must have."

The hallway is cleaner than he remembers it being, the stairs are too. Outside the air is surprisingly fresh, a shy blue sky and silvery puddles, a buzzing delivery trike unloading at the tech store across the street, a blonde woman on the sidewalk in a golden raincoat, the woman smiles directly at them, big white smile and "Sheridan," Marfa snaps, "get lost," tugging Max in the opposite direction, up the street and away.

MINOS DOC title TK production notes/personal

This whole thing feels like a big mistake.

People keep saying, Oh you're so lucky, you're at the center of everything that's going on, no filter! But nothing is going on. Fux says, You don't get it Serge, Minos is like a saint, he's changing the world! Tf am I supposed to say to that? changing it into what? I told Fux I can't make a meet with Minos happen, they are not happy about that.

Even people who don't buy into the woo are like, Blast gig, you get to hang with Mister Minos, what's he like? I say, He's like the NDA I signed. Or they say, if you ever need a hand tell them to hire me, all that exposure, you know how many followers Mister Minos has on Kickchat?!! Yeah I know. I also know those followers post straight up fantasyland bullshit—Minos doesn't use his MePage, doesn't look at fan PowerShots or relink linkis, doesn't hook up on Twistie, no matter how many fake videos people post it does not happen. And Minos and Regon don't do juice fasts, or any kind of fasts—Regon's always got a cigar and an espresso, where do people even get this shit—and they don't go up on rooftops at night to pray or dance around or whatever.

The days actually go like this: Minos is heads-down with his beats, Regon's in and out of meetings, interviews, parties, I said to him, So you just don't sleep? and he says, Oh Dark Park cured my insomnia, but there's a lot going on. Sorin's dealing with logistics, merch, the Indigo label guy, Quest Fest, whatever else is happening. At this level there's always an ecosystem, but they go light, no friendtourage or fuck toys. Sorin's got a remote liaison, their handle is Unicorn16, who runs a plug-in crew, and there's agency security that changes out every few days.

What the celebrity means at my end is always needing to navigate crowds and situations, it gets intense, gets like worship—like those antler drag people, and the flower brigade, they get in everywhere, sticking flowers in weird places, and the Horny Nights mosh bros always half-ass naked, and that freak with the drone, someone needs to have a talk with that dude—plus the security, and passwords that keep changing. Unicorn16 gave me contractors' clearance to save hassle, except at Sum Audio they passed thru Minos and Regon but they kept scanning my tag till I finally said Is this because your scanner's suddenly fucked or I'm Black or what.

Plus it's always a struggle to get any usable B-roll of Minos and Regon. Last night in the hotel hallway, I'm going for cute couple stuff, nothing intrusive, but Minos is really pushing back, like No fucking way—contractually I have access, but I'm not going to alienate the talent, so I back off, go down to the lobby bar. Sorin's camped under this candy-pink spot like a space ray, talking to some woman in a garage full of white dust, like a haunted house or a coke explosion, big metal armature behind her. Sorin says, Sergey, this is Suze and her maynad (??) sculpture, Suze, this is Sergey, our recording angel. I say, Don't know about the angel part, and Sorin and Suze the sculptor both smile, like Aw, he's clueless. This fucking woo vibe! It's like a filter came down and that's all they can see, a cult filter, except they're not destructive like a cult. Somebody, not me, could make a totally different film here, just about that aspect.

And none of it would bother me, none of it would even matter if the visuals were there, but they're not. They are NOT. No more Caravaggio, just this backstage vérité, Warhol or Tillmans, but minus any bad behavior. So what am I shooting, what am I even doing here.

Today's a travel day, Friday is on-site/VIP, Saturday is the show. Maybe performance will bring up the overall energy, or I'll salvage what I can in post. Either way it's over, chalk it up to whatever, and I'm out.

***

Long day on-site.

Starts with Regon and the LD and camera crew chiefs, those new GeniuScope decks they're using are crazy!! But most of it is proprietary. So I'm over to Sorin and the backstage manager touring the fenced-off luxury tents, the dedicated VIP entry looks like a kill floor chute, Sorin says, Do you use Backdoor or One Way for your scans? When the site supervisor takes us up on the DJ tower they put in just for Minos, he's showing her the polycarb walls and sight lines—the view is great, full 360 on the grounds—but she's asking about a lock-and-block moat. Supervisor says, I guarantee this build is secure.

I'll plug into Minos's board and use the tower rigging for ambient mics, and there're perimeter facilities for vendors and lavs, I can shoot crowd pick-ups from there if I need to. Regon makes a point of telling the site team heads that I'm Minos's exclusive shooter, access all areas, not just stage and backstage but anyplace I want to go, he says, Make sure all your security's onboard with that. Then he says, Sergey is a famous filmmaker, Sergey made Ace or Deuce—Seriously, Ace or Deuce?! Ace or Deuce that I shot run and gun with that cokemonger Alistair, who spent half the opening blowing the gallery director which I also shot, until the gendarmerie showed up and padlocked the place with us in it, seriously THIS is the one Regon likes?!!

After Sorin leaves, for once Regon's not in a hurry, he says, Want to eat? Uni sent over a pedigrill, green chili rolls and Limonale. Regon never had Limonale before, he's like Here's to new experiences! and almost chokes it's so sour. He laughs, I laugh, then because I can't not say it, I say, Every other film I shot is better than *Ace* or *Deuce*, I can show you. He says, I want to see them. But that one reminded me a lot of Max's shows, Max Caspar, you know who that is?

By now I do. In between not getting footage I'm doing more homework, about Minos playing mid-level clubs and little streetfests before he met Regon, Minos never officially played at Dark Factory but he and Regon did some type of fucked-up rave on the roof there that shut the club, like completely shut it down, wish I could have shot that! That's where Felix Perez turned into Minos, with the mask, like ground zero for the woo, and shit's been ramping up ever since, there are threads as long as books about it, by people hit like Fux is hit. The Silver Landings event has all type of fan videos, big wet dream vibe, and videos of the mural (met Derek Ferris at an opening once, all I remember is him asking did I know the people who ran the Berlinale). And the AltFest9000 mess, everybody heard about that, the producer had to pay some bigass fine, long threads about that too. But there's no video for Max Caspar, nothing except random art school stuff, and some footage from a show he put on where a building burned down. And if I'm being hardcore objective, I can see there's some linkage, visual linkage, between that and *Ace* or *Deuce*.

And I can also see that Regon really wants to talk about Max Caspar. Still the party king with his diamond studs and Ivy Meow hoodie, but he's quiet, just sitting on those bleachers, firing up a cigar, the smoke's hanging over his face like a caul, or a perfect post effect. And I'm thinking, What's all this like, for Regon? I never look at subjects that way, I'm there to see and to shoot, but right then I'm thinking, what's it like to be like that, be global but be himself too, a dude who came out of a divey underground scene? And then he starts talking, still quiet, he says, Max is my friend for a long time, he's not like anybody else I ever met, he mostly lives in his own world. Sometimes you can't even talk to him! But Max sees into things, Max is the only one who saw this coming, everything that's happening. You know what I mean?

And I'm thinking, so do we talk about the woo? Minos is already spooky, and Sorin, she's selling and buying. But Regon, this is his show, no way he believes. So I don't say anything.

And he shrugs, and I see there was more, way more, I should have said something, mistake but it's too fucking late, now he's asking, What's your movie called, what's the title? And when I shake my head, like Doesn't have one, he toasts me with the Limonale can, it flashes gold in his hand, he says, Tell me when it does. Me and Felix are off for a little, see you at the party.

***

"What's that smell," Felix kneeling naked by the tub, "is it soap?" and "Scent dispenser," Ari nudging with one toe a floating plastic waterlily, its perfume too sweet like the water is too warm, in this soaking tub squared like the black skylight overhead, its pane puddled with the rain that worried Meghan, *What if it's still pouring tomorrow?* but *Let it,* Felix said back, flat, and that was that. Beside the tub is a black hotel tray, bulb glasses and a bottle of Albariño, and a nearly-full can of espresso: Delirious Girl just sent a case, they want to create a branded blend just for Ari, it makes him think of the cases of NooJuice in the Factory, no one drinks NooJuice anymore. He reaches for the bottle, but Felix shakes his head, so "You want a shot of B? Or we'll grab a drink downstairs, at the VIP thing."

"VIP, jesus. They'll be all over the place tomorrow—"

"We don't need to stay long. One drink."

"—your paparazzi too. Celebrity documentary—"

"'Actualities,' that's what documentaries used to be called, Sergey told me that. Sergey's a good guy."

"He's your guy, not mine," Felix frowning, sinking in, letting the water cover him. "Once he's gone, I'll play you what I've got for LAB. Once all this is over—"

"Let's just do this, now," brushing the damp hair from Felix's forehead, reaching below that water to stroke him, Felix sighs. Felix is barely dealing with Quest Fest, insisting on tablet-only interviews, blowing off this welcome party even though VIP access is in the contract; Felix is even more focused, fixated, on the beats for his new event, not a festival or even a performance, maybe they should call it an actuality? this LAB that Felix says has to be completely private but also accessible—how, Y? live? some other way?—in a little church at the top of a little mountain, stone stairs and a metal skyway tram that looks a thousand years old, that tram must be giving Meg nightmares. But Meg plows on, negotiating with the church people, looking to Ari to translate what Felix wants, then tell her what comes next, Meg always relies on him to know what comes next . . . He does not know, he feels the itch of his scar as the plastic flower floats and bumps against his back. "This is nice, right? We should get a tub like this at our place."

"And where's that? our place?" and before Ari can answer "We're married, but we don't even have a place to live—it's like Genie, it's worse than Genie! We can't even go out for food anymore—"

"It's OK," knowing Felix is thinking of that taverna, the ambush by the server and her friends, eight, ten, more surrounding them, grabbing linkis then grabbing onto Felix, he tried to make them stop but they would not stop, he had to hot-button security to get out, the last thing he saw was that server, on her knees on the entryway tile, sobbing. "We can take a break, and look for a place. You work too hard anyway—"

"It's not the work, I can handle the work. I just, I have to keep up with it—"

"Keep up—"

"You know what this is! You know—"

"Felix, it's OK," insistent past the sense, dry and rising, that Felix is somehow right, that no one can keep up with this, that they will hit some point—will it be MinosLAB?—where they finally fall, into a space so big that even the spin will not hold them, the fall that takes Felix, takes them all the same way those dancers took him, right down to the ground, and what happens then? Max might have the words for it, is that why he avoids seeing Max? Is that why he used to feel that he and Felix would never have enough time together? not the old sad ache but this new true fear—

"—it's what we wanted, everything we wanted," one hand clenched unconscious to his chest, his heart, *it's in us too, can you hear it?* "And once all this is over—"

"We're not over," his own hand unlocking those clenching fingers, his mouth to Felix's mouth, throat, chest, nipples, tender then not, teeth and fingers and their wet bodies moving, sliding, grinding, bucking, the water splashing, sloshing, the can of espresso upended and floating, adding its oily darkness to that water, the rain drumming the skylight harder and harder as Felix cries out, as his wrist with the bone bracelet digs hard into Ari's skin, so hard it breaks the skin, so hard that blood threads the water too. Then Felix sleeps, instant, exhausted, head back against the tub's edge as Ari reaches for the wine bottle, to swallow, and swallow, and stare up at the skylight, out into the dark.

And when Felix climbs from the tub with a tired kiss, Ari dresses, black on black, and heads down to the hotel mezzanine where a woman with a glitter-streaked ponytail and a Quest Fest badge spots him at once, her smile half-welcome, half-relief—"Oh, you're here! I'm Bettye, head of hospitality, we spoke—" steering him under a giant stylized gold compass, the Quest Fest logo, to a roped-off cocktail area where hotel staff pop and pour mid-price champagne, she hands him a golden glass. "And can I get one for Mister—"

"He's getting prepped for tomorrow," his own smile to take the edge off, not his edge, downing that glass then taking up another as he eyes the other guests, the milling VIPs and the DJs talking gear, who does he know here? a few of those DJs, Angel Voom from Tbilisi, Clarence Kiz from Detroit, and Futuro in a vinyl hoodie scowling in his direction, Futuro keeps trying to beef with Felix who has no idea Futuro exists. An A&R in a white fur ball cap waves to him and beelines, but "Tomorrow's a big day," from a voice already at his elbow, dark goatee, tuxedo jacket and impeccable slashed jeans. "I'm Jase, from Insomnious. I was just about to grab a smoke, join me?" offering one of a pair of cigars. "Cohiba Reserva, a guy in Madrid gets them for me."

The white lights sparkle on the empty smoking patio, the rain has paused, and "I was hoping to meet your husband tonight," says Jase from Insomnious, chunky gold lighter in hand, the smoke tastes of bourbon and dry spice, of deliberate luxury. "You and I met already, at Dark Factory. Through a mutual friend," so is Jase a party guy, or an investor, someone Jonas once brought him in to hustle? He says nothing, lets the silence hang until Jase finally smiles, acknowledging the power of that silence, and "I streamed Dark Park with another mutual friend," showing his phone, *Call it MinosWorld, MinosLand, all beats no meat!* the message from a grinning black cat, who is that? "I had some expectations going in, but Mister Minos totally exploded them. Exploded me. And put me back together."

Still he says nothing, cautious now, the hard money vibe is definitely here but Jase wants something else too, wants Felix, what for? something he does not understand and "Insomnious did the CUE feed for Annexation 2.0, and the Grotto experience for 24Live, you might have seen those. Now we're dreaming up a new performance platform exclusively for Mister Minos. Without all the extras," Jase waving his cigar hand at the patio, the hotel, the festival, at him? "It seems like Mister Minos isn't really into extras, and he should have conditions exactly the way he wants them, so he can bless us with his energy. Tom—he's my business partner—he's in Warsaw, he'll jump right in if we can talk tomorrow—"

"We're talking right now," sending a puff of smoke into the mist: those white diamond drops, that black cigar and the wet black tips of his boots, the gold lighter and Quest Fest compass and champagne, all of it seeming to say something he does not understand either, an uneasy, unmoored feeling, is this the way Max used to feel when the Factory turned his world to Y? right before their world blew up? "And Felix doesn't really do after-parties—"

"I know. But you do," with a smile, showing his teeth, Jase's teeth are very white. "I can send a précis, or we can go granular, however you want to do this. Because we do want to do this, Mat Bergeron wants to do this. And I totally believe Mister Minos will too."

Bergeron? Bergeron is the grinning cat? recalling the days right before Dark Park, all those messages from Bergeron to Felix, *don't know how much a GOD player you were ha ha ha*, messages Felix did not answer so he did, what had he said to Bergeron? *He's got some weird theories about Felix,* he said that to Max—

—as the sky abruptly opens, another chilly gush, it drives them both back under the awning and "No inclement weather," Jase says, still smiling, "in Minosworld," as Ari reaches for the door, stepping from one darkness into another.

And later, while their room's half-draped windows frame a frail white dawn, Felix sleeps, but he lies dry-eyed and awake, still held by that same unease, finally climbing much too early from bed to drink scorched room service coffee and check his phone: Kickchat full of escalating babble, a MePage alert warning that his spillover page *Currently exceeds enhanced hosting limits*, a folder from Uni full of interview pleas and post-Fest invitations, messages from Meg at her most crisp because Meg is clearly upset, *Ops is NOT being helpful*—he should ask Meg about Bergeron, Bergeron is friends with Clara, has Bergeron been in touch with her?—and from Ilias thrilled that *Forking Paths ★★★★★ on Hey Listen AND ZiggyCast, tell Felix CONGRATS!!!* But he does not tell Felix that, or about Jase and Minosworld either, it feels wrong not to tell him about Jase, wrong that he even hesitates, how can he hesitate to say anything at all to Felix—

—who wakes unusually late and unusually silent, silent still when they finally arrive on-site, late there too, Felix in an oversized black hooded anorak like a monk's robe, Ari in a red Kaveman suit with bright dogged slashes of gold eye shadow, to find the grounds a swamped and spongy mess, and the crowd wet and fervent and aggressive, half of them wearing Mister Minos t-shirts or light-up antlers or both, one girl waves a homemade banner that reads ECSTASY & RUIN. Meg is already closeted with Ops, with even more things to be upset about: the DJ tower has intermittent feed issues, the playbill scan is scrambled and people are screaming on the site app—*where's the Minos bonus track???? Scheiße! Paid xxtra $$ but it wont even load? THIS IS FUKKED QUEST FEST IS FUKKED*—and the VIP list is porous with new, unvetted names, while the local cappies keep butting heads with venue security over turf.

Only Sergey seems completely unfazed, Sergey calm and shooting, keeping pace beside them and today's security detail, three men not burly but so solid they seem made of something denser than flesh, as they detour by the empty, windstruck VIP and greenroom tents, toward the cluster of hastily swapped-in trailers and RVs, past a hurrying scatter of staff, a journo interviewing a shivering pair of dancers beside some sponsor's neon logo, WHEEL INTO FLAVOR! and a stage runner herding a bedraggled Futuro—Futuro apparently just off his own rainy set, Futuro talking shit about Felix all day long on Beat Buzzer—Futuro who suddenly halts right in their path, phone in hand, and "Better put on your Halloween mask," his sneer to Felix and to his screen, as the runner tries to tug him away. "I just *killed* out there!"

"You need to step back," the lead security agent positioning himself in front of Felix, the other agents flanking him, angling Ari off to one side. "Step back, and cool down—"

"Fuck you, I'm not talking to you!" the phone shoved now to Felix's face. "I'm talking to this motherfucker—"

"Step *back*—"

"I got this, I got this!" a site guard with a stun baton shoving between the lead agent and Futuro, while a starry-eyed staffer? volunteer? fan? rushes out of nowhere to thrust at Felix a glittery bundle, crying "We know you love these! We love you!" Futuro swats at that bundle, the site guard reacts, overreacts, knocking Futuro to the muddy ground, barely missing Ari with the buzzing baton—

—and Felix as if suddenly awake jerks away from them all, a reflex move, a street move, grabbing Ari to haul him to the closest RV, Sergey sprinting beside them, Felix yanking hard at the unlocked door, "*In*, get in—"

—and "Minos?" from just past that door, Insomnious Jase startled off his phone, "Minos, is everything all right?" because this is not the headliner trailer or the greenroom RV but the VIP RV, low black sofas and golden trays of sushi and fruit, a suited bartender below a stage feed monitor, a suddenly staring crowd. The security agents clamber in, the lead agent saying urgent to Felix "Sir, sir you can't *do* that!" as Jase plucks up a plush black bar towel to offer to Felix, Felix wipes rain from his face, Jase murmurs something in his ear—

—something that Ari cannot hear, because Ari is still somehow sidelined, only watching, clutching that bundle that he sees, now, is a bouquet, was a bouquet, ripped glitter paper and half-smashed purple blooms, a muddied card scrawled in purple ink, *WE R UR FLOWERS.*

TOUCH THE SKY DOC production notes/personal

Sending selects to Regon now.

***

Nothing from Regon. Not this is great, or this is shit, or Minos hates it, nothing.

***

Still nothing from Regon. Fucking RESPOND.

***

Nothing. Put together more selects—the start of the first track, some crowd pans, Minos throwing the headphones—and sent them today.

This footage, everything I edited so far, it's the best thing I ever did. The rain, the dark, lime green sensor spots over the bleachers, phone lights everywhere, sparklers, light-up antlers, LD's totally erratic, firing 1-2-3 like cluster bombs, neon pink and gold, then nothing, then 1-2-3 1-2-3, the cams kept cutting in and out too. Only thing that never failed was the sound, beats like nothing I ever heard, not Dark Park or

Forking Paths—Minos was in some other headspace up there, beyond ruthless, fucking barrage, BPM ramping up and up like he's revving the gears of the universe. I got him looking at Regon right as the intro dropped, like the last minute he knew he was on earth with other people.

And Regon's dancing, no matter what he just kept dancing, sweating, gold make-up all over his face—crowd was hyped for that, big rockstar cheer when they saw he was up there with Minos. Not like they needed any hyping, from the drop they're foaming, flags, flowers, guys ripping off their shirts, people booing too and scuffling, security's more and more visible. By then I was shooting on backup, bars were getting low but somehow I wasn't stressed about it, I knew it would last and it did.

Then people started overrunning the barriers, like waves smashing into the shore, smashing into each other, in the mud, crying, trying to climb the boom lift riser, some of them made it halfway up, a few almost got to the top, what if those people were able to pull Minos out??!! When Minos threw the headphones they really started fighting, cherrypicker's bucking and jerking, I'm thinking is this driver even able to operate this thing right now?? so when he crashed the first barricade I wasn't even surprised. Got past the second barricade, security bodywrapped us into a cop van like we're getting bagged, Regon is telling me, Stop, stop shooting, and Minos says to him, like they're alone—I could barely hear him, the crowd was so loud—Minos says, That's it, done, I'm done. Then a cop pulled me back out, the van took off, and there's a site escort in a club cart screaming, Where to? where to?! so I say, Wherever Meghan Sorin is, take me there. Getting thru those grounds—I did crisis training for street shooting, Y sessions where they put you into riot situations, but this is not that, this is actual chaos. I couldn't even shoot, had to hold on with both hands to the fucking cart.

Meghan's in the green room RV, watching it all on the monitor. I was shook af and so was she, she just kept saying, I'm so glad about the tower, I'm so glad that tower held. I told her about the cop van, what Minos said, and she started crying, she says, Why is this happening, I did everything, I don't understand. Finally another escort showed up to get us offsite, back to the hotel. She says, I cannot work right now, and I know I'm not going to sleep, so she ordered a bottle of Cîroc and a tray of pommes frites and we sat in her room and drank, we never did eat the frites. She told me about the whole Maenad thing, how it felt to be under those trees at Dark Park, feeling the heat of the fire but feeling like the fire couldn't touch her, touch any of the women, because they all felt invincible, she said, We were invincible, I understood what Suze was doing, in that moment I understood everything.

And I told her that I understood too, I could finally see what everybody means, her, Fux, everybody—the woo, the burning bush, it's there, I see it. And she said, I knew you would.

And I told her why I chased this gig so hard, because I needed so much to shoot something worth seeing, worth showing people, maybe I was yelling by then but I said I need to keep shooting, I know my contract ends tonight but I need to keep shooting! She said, Only Ari can authorize that. I said, He said to tell him when the film had a title, well it's got one now, *Touch the Sky*, will you tell him that? She said, When he answers me.

Around 6am, she fell asleep in the armchair, I turned off the lights and left. I haven't smoked in 5 years but I bummed a cigarette off a lobby barista, a Marlboro Gold, and I sat on the smoking patio and scrolled thru everything tagged Quest Fest, my shoulder was starting to hurt like fuck. Around noon Meghan messages, she says, Ari hasn't answered. We have to leave, where do you want your flight to go?

So I'm home. I edit, I watch Brakhage, Greaves, Kirsten Johnson, Ahmed Bondy, I do PT and get the shots for the shoulder spasms, my arm still feels like it's going to fall off from how I had to situate myself out of Minos's way, the 3 of us jammed in that tower. Meghan says she and Suze watched *Constructive Panic*, they thought it was great. But *Touch the*

Sky is past all that, *Touch the Sky*'s not telling people what they're seeing, or trying to shape what they see. *Touch the Sky* is actual sight.

I posted AWAY on my MePage, but people keep contacting me for interviews, gigs, all that "exposure," fuck all that, I already have a gig! I might be spiraling a little here but I'm not wrong, I saw it, I see it, I have to finish it, <u>this has got to get done.</u>

***

Climbing blinking from the Hopper into a wash of late afternoon sun, opposite a curbside line of contractors' vehicles parked halfway down Neuberg Street, outside "The Dream Hotel," Marfa says to Max. "Remember the first time we came here?"

"I remember," that day's cold blue sky, the milling tourists and their guide taking pictures of the big black doors with the gear-shaped handles: now those doors are gone, are glass, the front wall is all glass, all the Dark Factory signage is stripped away, like an old friend barely recognizable. "It's a hotel, now?"

"In process. Hotel, two restaurants, entertainment, the fourth floor's going to be members-only suites for the high rollers. Big bucks, Siegler must be crying in jail. Or laughing."

Jonas Siegler is in jail? "Why are we here?"

"Because I wanted you to see that things change."

"I know things change," squinting up at what was once the roof, Marfa was there then too, holding tight to his arm in the cold. Now she stands in the sun, pointing to what used to be the performers' entrance, the awning is gone, the door is a wall and "Wasser and Wassermann," she says, "won't win any Pritzkers for it, but the build foreman's giving us a private tour," yet what is there to see? *You hate the Factory, you love the Factory,* he shakes his head.

She shrugs, looks back to the building, at him again, then "OK, then—Wait, hang on," with a little smiling frown, tapping her ear, the tiny black feedline that runs to her phone. "I need to grab this."

To give her privacy he turns away, walks away, slowly, like filing past the casket at a wake: electricians' trucks and carpenters' vans, a hulking black-paned generator, the irregular thumping of nail guns—until he stumbles, one foot encircled by a thick snaking cable as "Sidewalk's closed!" a worker calls from behind the orange barricade. "Construction zone, see the signs?"

"Right," righting himself, this awkward body, stopping to consider that worker: scratched hardhat and reflective vest and belt with mysterious tools, every detail as detailed as an NPC, and "Did you ever go here?" he asks the worker. "When it was Dark Factory?"

"It was what?"

"Never mind," turning back up the block, back to Marfa who is still on her phone, whoever she talks to is making her smile, a lipstick smile as glossy as her hair: Marfa is growing hard to recognize too, so entirely engaged, so at home in this world as he is not—even now, when the changes he and Ari enabled are gaining stranger strength, another world or worlds emergent from the one that has gone, broken and scrambling into being, every visit shows him that—still he remains apart, a moon of a man. But around his finger is the ring she gave him, ouroboros unchanging, *I'll be here* and she always is: asking the questions he wanted most to answer, riding shotgun through Dark Park, making sure he still sees the sun, Marfa is always there for him—

—as her call finally ends and her smile changes, a certain glow receding as she faces him again, why? and "You want to go to Cheap Breakfast?" he asks. "My treat."

"You still know what money is, cool. No, I need to do this tour, but I'll walk you over there," heading brisk down the block, he has to stretch to keep up. "So I heard Clara's got some new hires on the string, maybe you heard that too?" new hires? to do what? He has not heard that and does not care, so "Who were you talking to?" he asks instead, yet instead of an answer she gives him a look, brief and wholly indecipherable—

—as they turn the corner into flat and sudden glare, sun flash from storefront windows, Marfa's glare as sudden—"Do I have to put a stalker tag on you, Sheridan?"—as the blonde woman in the golden raincoat appears on the sidewalk like a clumsy cut-in, this time in a black mesh blazer and boots and "You won't respond to messages," Sheridan says, deliberate and bright. "So this is the only way—"

"No, the 'only way' is for you to—"

"Max," aiming that smile now at him, "I'm Sheridan Mikelson, I work for Leon Cardenal—"

"—leave Max alone, because—"

"—Leon is interested in your artistic development—"

"—Max is completely *not* interested—"

"—but Marfa refuses to introduce you to Leon. Even though she could have. Did you introduce him to Bee Boy, Marfa?"

"Fuck *off*," Marfa taking his arm in a custodial grasp, marching directly toward Sheridan who must finally step aside, he watches through the smudged glass door as Sheridan waves at him, then departs as "Water," Marfa says, perched on the edge of a booth. "Two."

Cheap Breakfast is not crowded, only a few desultory counter customers, more NPCs, and their server is quick. But it still seems long to Max as they sit in that human silence, Marfa's silence, until he lifts his glass and finally asks, "What does Leon Cardenal want me for?"

"Use you for a joystick, probably. Leon's all about games and Y now, he's over 2D art since that mural guy told him to beat it. And Sheridan's his lackey, in case you couldn't tell."

"Who's Bee Boy?"

Her look changes, indecipherable again, then "His name is Pavel. He owns an apiary," showing on her phone a man standing beside a wooden gate with a bright yellow sign, HIVE MIND: work pants, red beard, shy wide smile. He takes the phone, to examine that smile more closely, but it automatically swipes to the next photo, in this one Pavel is shirtless beside a plywood bed, the plywood bed in the Sugar Shack space, in the next one—"Oh," he says. "He's your, he's—"

"Max—"

"You don't have to say anything," feeling the twinned stings of jealousy and dismay, beside a deeper, sadder gladness, Marfa should have a man who brings her sweetness, a man fully of this world, *love is a wonderful thing, things change.* "He looks like, like a nice guy."

"He is. And you can meet him anytime you want. Except not in the game, Pavel doesn't play games."

"I bet not."

She reaches across the table to press his hand, the hand with the ring, then "I really need to take that tour," she says. "You'll get back OK?"

"I'll be fine."

"Remember, don't talk to Sheridan. Or to Leon—"

—and she is up from the table and out the door, he sees the breeze sudden in her hair, like Mila riding away on the blue bike: because Marfa owns her own velocity, *I always find people to talk to, Max I can do this* and she can, she does, she will. And in a year, ten years, a hundred, however long anyone will ever need or want to learn about Dark Factory, what it is or was or means, she is the one they will read, her interviews, her stories of this story, McSq2—

—so maybe he ought to go, too, and this time stay gone, what can this outside world, physical world, offer to him, mean to him, anymore? Maybe he ought to find Davide, Davide and his trapdoors and many intersecting worlds, network-based, self-teaching, knowledge-sharing organisms, like a swarm of rootlets, a flock of birds; Davide has a handle in the game now, Hand-Painted Fool, a bucket for a head and Catastrophia wings. Maybe Davide has finally found some way to make that fully playable human character, maybe this game can remake him one last time—

"—refill, here?" the server leaning in with water pitcher in hand, condensation dripping, the diamond sparkle of those drops, he touches one, feels its tiny transitory cold. "Or did you want to order? Vegan chili cheese fries are on special today."

At the thought of eating, his stomach contracts, but this booth owns a kind of distant comfort, the booth he and Ari sat in that very first night, *just say if the Factory's real or not.* So "Black tea?" that arrives hot in a little white pot, with a side saucer of golden honey, Bee Boy, Pavel in Marfa's bed, her warmth and her heat . . . How long has it been, for him? another abdication of the physical, *I don't really have a sex life now,* another memory of Ari with the

Super Pleasure Pak, and Not Dog where he gave Ari his notes, proto notes, *Lost in the Stars, Fuck the Factory* but the Factory is fucked forever now, the Factory is gone, that roof enclosed where he saw those stars, does Ari know about all that?

And where is Ari? Mathias says that Ari and Felix have disappeared, Mathias is bereft, and beyond fury at Quest Fest, *Their management had duty of care! Minos was in danger, actual danger, none of this is Minos's fault! Their management should be sued into DIRT*—but from everything Mathias told him, and the few videos he saw, Quest Fest seemed to operate like a preordained rite: the blind dancers surrounding the elephant, tugging on its trunk, inhaling its breath, overwhelmed by its weight, *this is my body, religion has always been a shuck,* Mathias said that too, Mathias who has seen religious extremism before, Mathias saw first what they would all want Felix to be. And Felix bears the brunt of it all in a way he does not, even Ari does not, where is Ari's place in this new world—

—and he reaches for a wrinkled paper napkin, smooths it flat enough to write on, the faithful pen from his old satchel, **At Cheap Breakfast. Where are you?** then takes a picture and sends that picture to Ari. Pouring the teacup full, he sips, scalds his lip, sucks at the pain while he waits for an answer, while the booths around him fill and empty, people chat and argue and laugh, the streetlights past the windows shine bright as Sheridan's smile.

TOUCH THE SKY DOC production notes/personal

Last night Fux hit me up, first thing I say is, You're right, it's real. They say, Finally! How's your movie? I say, Movie's not done, and Regon and Minos took off somewhere, no one knows where. And they say, Blazey, you know Blazey? the booker? Blazey just told me, top secret but Minos is in New York.

***

Haven't couch surfed for years, but Phadrea is cool, she says, Santi told me you're in big need, so mi foldout su foldout, just don't drink out the coffee or the rum. Phadrea runs the floor at House of Hello, so I can work at night, then head over to Café Comida when she comes home.

Minos and Regon are a train ride away. But I don't go over there, I don't even go to the neighborhood.

Regon still hasn't responded, he's not engaging with anything, any of the mess people put out there, everybody's got an opinion and the less they know the more they talk. Even people from back in the day, some guy who knew Regon from the Holy Roman Empire thing, that guy will not shut up, and some girl who started a Fundalot because Minos caused her "aural distress," she's getting money for it too. Or punkass Futuro's diss track video, makes himself look like a badass and Minos look out of it, fucking preschool edit job, then all the remixes of that. And the hit piece Revealer did, that piece has <u>nothing</u> to do with anything that actually happened.

Meghan says Regon won't talk about that, or about the gig that's supposed to be happening next, whatever it is, MinosLAB. She showed me some pictures of Regon in a kitchenette, being hugged on by this little lady in a flowered sweatshirt, she says, This is what he wants to talk about now, meeting Felix's mum.

So Meghan talks to me, she says, All I do is report to lawyers and placate that monsignor, the church wants another site deposit, I have no idea if I should send that or not. She says, I thought I was part of this too, not just a business associate. She's spending more and more time on Suze's project, *The Artemis Wilderness* (found out Suze used to be partners with Karagiannis? how she and Meghan met). Suze was planning to do a sculpture of Minos, but after Dark Park she made that big metal Maenad instead—Maenad gets a charge-up from Minos/Dionysus, but doesn't follow him like in the myth, she follows Artemis into the woods, Maenad takes a walk in the dark park. Meghan showed me Suze's studio footage, I said, Well no shade but it's stiff af, really should be reshot. I know she wants me to do it, but I'm not shooting anything right now, haven't even touched my rig since QF. Like being stranded in midair, the way a cartoon character falls off a cliff, time stops so they can look into the camera, like What tf just happened? You can only fall for so long.

If I asked Regon about how he saw *Ace* or *Deuce* in the first place, would he answer me? Or about why he wanted us to meet in that game? Or about what he almost said, on the bleachers?

If I could talk to him now, if he would listen, I'd just say <u>Look at the footage</u>. If he sees it, I can finish, and everybody will see, see that they're all in the dark, just a hurricane of sparks, all those people under the cherrypicker, and in the VIP trailer, and the high school kids down the block at the Shake Out, and the bodega guy rearranging his stock, all of them, all of it, all the time. Maybe I should get on that J train, go and talk to Regon, go and say look at it, just fucking <u>look and see</u>.

***

The church's windows are bright as anime, drenched blues and glowing yellows, a jumble of symbols and figures that to Ari mean nothing but "That's St. Francis," says Jenni, gold hoop earrings and oversized sports jersey, pointing up, "and that one's St. Joseph," a man in a dress with a handful of lilies, *the ultimate club flowers,* so is Joseph the patron saint of clubbing? He thinks of the church in Barcelona, and the church on top of that mountain, Meg keeps asking if MinosLAB is still in play but he has not answered her because there is no answer: only escalating promises from Insomnious Jase, promises made only to Felix, details shared only with Felix, Jase the true believer calling Felix all the time, Felix tells him almost nothing about those calls. But still he knows that Jase is wrong, and MinosLAB is wrong, wrong and hazardous, not able to say how he knows, and would Felix even listen—

"—for Saturday Masses, I play keyboard. Not the big organ, I'm not a star like this one," nodding to Felix approaching up the side aisle, Felix in anorak and ASTER BAR cap, unshaven, on edge, forcing a smile as "Hey, Jenni," Felix says. "Ari, this is Jenni, we went to school together. Jenni, do you know if Mrs. G.—"

"We went *everywhere* together. School trips, parties," as Ari pictures teenage Felix, what would it have been like to know him then? to dance with him? "And we both took lessons from Mrs. G., he was Mrs. G.'s pet. You heard Mrs. G. had a stroke?"

"What? No. Is she all right? Is—"

"She went real quick," Jenni making the Catholic cross sign, Felix staring at her, then at the stone floor. "So you're visiting your mama? Are you going to play one of your shows here, your crazy DJ shows?"

Felix says nothing, his silence hangs in the silence of the church until "Felix's mom," Ari says, "is a total sweetheart. We—"

"Got to go," Felix abrupt and turning away, Ari quick beside him down the aisle and out to the vestibule with its stack of volunteer clipboards and blank-eyed statues of angels, exiting through the heavy double doors, Felix pausing to scan the block—no more hired security, Felix insists on that, security is part of everything he says he is done with though Meg was aghast, more urgent messages Ari had no idea how to answer, *What is Felix's thought process here? Unsafe for you both*—Felix tugging down his ball cap brim, hustling Ari with a fugitive's speed back to the apartment—

—where they have spent these last long weeks, weeks that feel to Ari like years, Felix's mother the only bright spot in the airless days: Ava Perez with arms open to gather in her son, opening again for Ari in a doubled embrace, her dark head barely reaching Ari's shoulder. Then *Sit*, at her tiny kitchen table, take-out napkins and bottles of vitamins, a bowl of peanuts, a plate of chocolate cake. *And tell me what's that on your face, since when do you have a beard?*

She asked no questions beyond the practical—Did Felix get the apartment keys? Did the cousin clean up the apartment?—toggling between their immediate well-being, slices of that cake and cups of strong Estrella coffee, and their future, a future that must include a church wedding, *Small, big, however you like I don't care. But get him a ring, Pio! Not a tattoo, a ring.*

Ink is more permanent than rings, Mom.

Pio? That's his nickname?

Escorpio, he's a Scorpio, you didn't notice? And you don't smoke that in here, you shouldn't be smoking at all.

I should probably quit, meekly tucking away the cigar, to bring Ava's nod in approval and Felix's astonished shrug, *How does she do it* . . . Ava is not beautiful as Felix is beautiful, but the family resemblance is strong, the same thick dark hair, same lift of the chin; Ava the nurturing mother and the steely firewall, shutting out the neighbors trying to peer at her notorious son, shutting down the family noise at the cousin's sudden displacement, *Whose apartment is it, hey? Who still pays the rent?*

—on this third floor space with its two dusty windows, grungy towels and ITS BABE TYME! lager banner over the door, the cousin's left-behind clothes pushed aside to make room for their own bags, though Ari felt a sweet initial thrill to see the globe lamp hanging over the bed, *I have that exact same lamp in my place,* Felix saw his smile and smiled at the memory too. But no smiles now for either of them, as "I'm really sorry about your teacher," Ari's hand on Felix's arm, "I wish I could have met her," trying to draw him closer, but Felix pulls away—"If I didn't know I was done before, I fucking would now . . . Need to get with Jase—" hunching on the sofa, reaching for his headphones—

—as Ari takes out his own phone, but only to scroll as he listens to Felix's side of the call: "Right, right," Felix agreeing, with what? to what? "I'll keep it tight, and—Right. Sending now," ending the call, headphones off, he looks to Ari, then, flat, "What."

"You're sending stuff to Jase? New stuff?"

"The stuff I've been working on, the LAB mix. I told you—"

"You told me you'd play it for me."

"I will, when you're open to it! To realigning the energy," Jase-speak that Felix speaks now, as if those words and concepts are his own, as if Jase is seeping into him. "If I hadn't imposed my own energy at Quest Fest, confrontational energy—"

"What you need is to get some downtime—"

"You sound like my mother," one hand pinching and twisting the sofa cover, some sports team's garish logo repeating in black and gold. "I'm fine. I'm just trying to keep going, keep us going—"

"You can do that without Insomnious," *I have to keep up, we do want to do this, Mister Minos will too,* do what, make what? in that lab in that church on that mountain, how far is that fall? "Their platform, whatever it is, we don't even know what it is—"

"I know! I'm taking care of it! Why can't you just—"

"Then tell me what's going on. Tell me—"

"—just fucking *trust* me!" Felix off the sofa and slamming into the only other room, the coffin-sized bathroom, as Ari stares out the window, seeing nothing, again, again—

—as their phones ping almost in tandem, both with more frantic messages from Ilias: ***Indigo is here 4 U!! always here 4 U!!*** and ***I pushed***

him way 2 hard, I get that! talk 2 me tell me what 2 do?? Then Felix's phone chimes alone, *Mama* on the ID and "Your mom," Ari calls, "your mom's calling," but only silence from behind that narrow door: he waits, waits, then leaves, sliding on cheap black shades like a cartoon disguise, lighting up on the stairs, the dry smoke in his mouth as he heads out and down the block—

—to walk, and walk, avoiding the dank rattling trap of the train, thoughts crowding and harrying him along, like all the calls he pushes off onto Meg, lawyers' updates about the Quest Fest lawsuit and the venue lawsuit and their own countersuits and counterclaims, *adverse impacts on career and professional reputation,* and the Futuro nuisance suit, toilet paper but it gets way too much play, gets Futuro the Beat Buzzer spotlight he craved; while they hang in the void, all the chasers running the other way to shield their own brand safety—though some have stayed, the hardcore fans, the serious and devoted, a few of the crazies; and some industry people, Upsetta, and Clarence Kiz, Lars Lindberg from AltFest, and most loudly and loyally Julian Zero, *Ari Regon always keeps it real and he always will!* And Indigo doubled down, tripled down, *Mister Minos is an avatar of change, whatever Mister Minos does we stand behind,* Indigo got slammed too in that knives-out Revealer piece, Ilias and Gussie called greedy enablers, and Felix a reckless diva getting high off his own supply. But the worst of it was aimed full-bore at him, *What disasters are left on Regon's to-do list? Besides the blatant attempt to deflect the dangerous crash and burn at Quest Fest with Mister Minos's instant so-called retirement? Wave goodbye as Mister Minos disappears forever into Regon's black hole ego—*

—walking faster, the blocks shifting from one vibe to another, this neighborhood he does not know but recognizes, restaurants with deadpan names like BUNNYHAUS and IT'S A DRIP, grated sidewalk trees and sneaker boutiques and snapcard kiosks and clubs dark and quiet in the daytime light, JELLYBAR and HOUSE OF HELLO, and KITTYTAT TATTOOS, *one in Brooklyn, one in D-dorf,* did Felix get a tattoo there? There are no Kaffee Karts that he can see, maybe there are no Kaffee Karts here, but he finds a place with a blue awning called BLUE AWNING and sits outside on a wobbly metal chair, to ignore his pour over and stare at his phone, if he messages will Felix answer? Is Felix talking to Jase again right now—

—then clicking away, back to Sergey's last message—he has not answered Sergey either, does Sergey think he is stonewalling? when really this is an echo of Max's notes, *I didn't answer you because I didn't know what to say*—this message one last clip, twenty-six seconds of tilt-a-whirl and screaming, a sudden cut to show a man's body falling, cutting back to his own face flushed and wild and gold, shouting something to Felix that the camera cannot hear, Felix's arm so tight around his shoulders that later there were marks, finger marks, Felix holding him and staring stark into the wet black sky, **Touch the Sky**, how many times has he watched this? though Felix refuses to watch, to see, Felix thinks he knows what happened and that all of it, the screaming, crashing, everything, is his fault—But this is on *him*, his job, always his job to stand at the center, Ari Superman, *Ari's a maker* but he can make nothing happen anymore or find that center either, the monster version of those long-ago Dreamtime days, no dream and no more time, his instinct smothered, his authority denied, he can only stand watching as Felix falters, as everything collapses—

"—Regon?" a woman looming over him now, red corkscrew curls, a staring friend in a kepi cap behind her. "I knew it! You're Ari Regon."

"Not today," up from the chair, thumbing a ride service called Jump while they circle him and grab linkis and "You're shorter than I thought," the friend leaning in, the smell of sweat and licorice, "but I'd still fuck you. You and me and Mister Horny, banging threeway—"

—and more of them camped on Ava's block, between GODDESS HAIR and a walk-in dentist with tagged-up metal shutters, a pack of teenage kids that spot then surround him, pressing in, one boy in a handmade Minos t-shirt keeps trying to jam something into his jacket pocket, while he stares straight ahead and leans on the buzzer, Ava's buzzer, until the door finally opens, he is inside, his hands are shaking.

But Ava does not mention those kids, or ask why he is here or where Felix is; instead she sets out a fresh cup of Estrella and a plate of spicy cheese biscuits, he eats one, eats another, how can he be this hungry without realizing it? and "Your family," she says, "they must be nice people. You're close to them? They'll come to the wedding?"

He thinks, first and oddly, of Jonas, then of his father, that sad apartment so much bigger than this one but so much less alive, does his father still live there? He never told his father about Felix. "Not that close to my dad. And my mom's not—around. Not for a long time."

"Well, Pio is your family now, we're your family . . . Tell me," folding her hands, a deep and searching urgency, "will you tell me what's happening to Pio?"

He tells her what he can, that the pace is brutal and the shows have been intense, sometimes insane, that Felix has changed—at this she nods, Felix's own firm nod, one, two—and Felix is isolating, *Mister Minos is unique but unique means only one,* with Jase in his ear like another kind of hum, he does not tell Ava about Jase but "I want," he says, "to keep him clear of that, all of that," feeling the dread that he cannot share, with her, with anyone, *If I'm done I'm dead.* "But he has to be able to play."

"His music—You're helping him?"

"I'm trying."

"You love him."

"More than anything."

"You'll take care of him. He's yours," so decisively that his eyes fill instantly with tears, hot on his cheeks, does Ava see? Ava reaching for his hand, squeezing tight, he can feel her ring, wedding ring, he squeezes back as hard as he can.

Then "Here," she says, rising, filling a paper bread bag with the rest of the biscuits, "take these home. And I'll walk down with you," standing arms crossed on the stoop while he exits, as if she will pounce on anyone who might try to pounce on him.

He takes the train back, stations rolling and lurching by, wedged into a doorside seat and watching another clip from Sergey, watching it again and again: the moments just before the first beat dropped, the camera aiming down and down through the flowers and the signs, the ecstasy and ruin, to the hundreds and hundreds of faces upturned in that rainy darkness, those faces could be from any dancefloor anywhere, every dancefloor everywhere, they exist in the spin, they *are* the spin, *everything we wanted*—

—and off the train, the shades left behind on the seat, to find at the end of their block another, smaller knot of kids, loitering outside the corner bodega: when they spot him they stare, hoot, hold up phones, and he walks straight toward them, toward what he needs—

—then up those other stairs again to find Felix back on the sofa, tense and drained, headphones in hand, but "The bodega lady says these will last two weeks," offering the bouquet, his bouquet, pink velvet roses and floppy greenery in a damp paper cone. And Felix almost smiles, Felix digs out an oversized beer mug for a vase, DIRTY DOG SHOTS'N'WINGS, silly and imperfect, and "Baby," Felix says. "Oh come here, baby—"

—to the tired little bed beneath the lamp's bright world, their own world, shaking that bed, their bodies fused and sweating, Ari's head on Felix's chest, the dandelion seeds in flight, Felix eyes-closed and murmuring, "All the dreams I had here—I dreamed of you, here . . . Jesus, Mrs. G. was right, we don't choose, but—What about the people who got hurt?"

"That's not on you. I should have said no to that tower, I should have told Meg—"

"What if that security asshole tased you? or you fell out of that fucking tower? And at Dark Park they jumped you! Like at the paper mill—"

"No one jumped me. It wasn't like that—"

"Genie, Silver Landings is what really split us up, right? And now she's gone. And Alaine, remember Alaine Majiic? She doesn't even play anymore. And I knew what was happening, I *knew,* but I just kept on—But MinosLAB could fix all that, fix the energy," sitting upright now, rubbing his face, the tufty bristles of his beard, his gaze on Ari's pleading for agreement, *you brought me, trust yourself, I do!* "Playing up there alone, just alone—You can see that, right?"

In answer he reaches for his phone, for that last clip, those faces, and "Look," he says, invites, insists. "Look at this, watch this. Watch all of it—"

—and Felix does as he says, watching once then again, again, another clip and another, Felix's own phone pinging, ignored on the floor until Ari picks it up, Bergeron is messaging, *Minos what's up, how are you??*

its ari hes good

Ari great to hear from you! QF what a clusterfuck, Minos really stirred them up

yeh

Really need to talk w/Minos about LAB

whats ur take on jase

Jason = too much Aztec WAY too much, can't be trusted, Nonstop found that out! Is Minos there, really need to talk

hes way busy rn, talk soon

—then ordering food, a double order of jackfruit wraps and curry noodle soup, Felix's eyebrows go up when he sees the bread bag—"Wait, those are my mom's?"—as Ari pulls on clothes for the Curb Chef delivery, adding a tip so enormous that the delivery runner stares through shaggy blond bangs, and "You like dance music?" Ari asks, taking the bags. "Where do you go to dance?"

"Dance? Uh, House of Hello, mostly."

"Maybe I'll see you there," with a smile, that smile flustering the delivery runner into a smile of their own, nervous and sweet and "Yeah," nodding, bangs flopping, "you, uh—Yeah!"

As Felix sits to eat in the table's clutter, containers and spoons and empty Delirious Girl cans, Ari takes up his own phone again to scan the map, where is House of Hello? not too far, he walked right past it, and every Wednesday is New Voices night. And Blaze the booker, Felix's old booker, has a high neighborhood rating on Beat Buzzer—

—as a new message arrives that makes him smile again, the smile only Max can call from him, *At Cheap Breakfast. Where are you?* Max off his beach somehow and writing on a wrinkled real-world napkin, Max the holy ghost, *you make your own heaven, I believe that* so he sends back a picture of the noodle bag, the mess and the roses, sends it with eight random seconds clipped from Sergey and his own message, *im here lets dance*

TOUCH THE SKY DOC production notes/personal

Regon watched it, Minos watched it.

We start shooting again next week.

so fucking ready

so happy

***

Mathias climbs like a crab, legs wide, body bent low to the sand between the twisting scrawls of the dune shrubs, and "Excellent new craftables," Mathias calls back, "the Floatsam crew's going to love them. Come on, I'll show you—"

—as a winged figure with a buckethead appears above them, circling over the lush treeline, a wobbly descent toward a yellow gingko tree just before the turn of the path. So "I'll find them," Max says, "the way a player would, just walking around."

"Canary always goes his own way," Mathias's shrug quick and annoyed. "Like Minos—And even if Click and Drag plan to buy the whole church, *and* that mountain, doesn't matter, it's still not going to work. Full stop, MinosLAB has got to be in here," Mathias more preoccupied than ever by his own grand unified theory, Felix's next show not just streamed but fully hosted within the game and only within the game, this plan at some kind of odds with the Insomnious plan, or platform, whatever that is; Ari had not explained it either but asked a question instead, *this cant happen but they really want it 2, can u school me??* on the labyrinth, that path debatably dating to the fifth century BCE, its whorls and switchbacks representing the journey of life and of the cosmos, the road for seekers, the human uterus, the eternal dancefloor, a shelter for monsters . . . Ari had also said *beach meet up* but his answer was equally direct, *No, real life*, or as close as they can come to it, he will sit in that dusty room that once was Ari's hideaway, *upstairs man*, and Ari will call, Ari is in New York now—

"—if Regon has some friction? He was asking about Jason Rice. You know Regon, what's his issue?"

He feels himself smile, a very small smile. "Ari? Ari wants to dance."

Mathias shows his green teeth in a smile too, is that a smile? then "Whatever. Happy hunting, check back with me at the foursquare,"

DARK PARK

049

Mathias's term for the quincunx, Mathias turning the opposite way, explorer's hat bobbing—

—and he waits, still watching the gingko tree, thinking of Bitter Lake, that little rowan copse, *it was a real world, you gave it everything* but everything he had was nothing like this, this *is* a real world, and how much does that owe to Davide's beloved MIW theory, world upon world, *after that is heaven, you believe in that?* Approaching slowly, as if toward a skittish animal, Davide on the ground now with dark wings twitching, the cartoon menace of his buckethead like something an angry teenager would draw, and "Greetings, pilgrim," Davide says as he nears, voice smoothed and adjusted, like a voice actor's. "Working hard for your boss?"

"Doing research. Outside research."

"Uh huh. Need to say thanks for that Valkyrie hookup, she's fucking great. Uber-geeked for flying lessons."

"Don't thank me," for Sheridan Mikelson: pursuing him into B of P, the one place Marfa never goes, Sheridan apparently stumbled over Davide instead, Davide a much better catch, stuffed with esoteric gaming knowledge, without a firewall and already on fire to meet a real catastrophe blonde. "Sheridan's got her own deal going on here, Marfa says—"

"Marfa," Davide fanning himself with one hand, middle finger pointedly pointed, "will never learn to fly . . . So I gave Jakka your trouble ticket," Jakka the UX master, Jakka one of the Solve for X stalwarts, Jakka who, Davide says, believes B of P has barely scratched the surface of its ultimate playability; strange to think that Mathias believes the same thing. "Insertion's not totally where he wants it to be, but Jakka's got a new workaround to try—full disclosure, it's buggy, and full disclosure he's been looking for another betanaut anyway."

"What happened to the first one?"

The bucket rattles, is that a laugh? "You got a timetable? You want to be here for Matty B's big launch?"

"I want to *be here*," with such simple blunt intent that "I'll tell Jakka," Davide says, "that you're go, he'll be in touch. And you tell

Clara," extending his wings, the snap of tautened leather, "I said to fuck cordially off the edge of the fucking betaworld. And keep some of that for yourself, pilgrim—I'm doing this for Jakka, not for you."

As Davide lifts off again, a steep and showy ascent, he turns back down the path: no way to predict what may or can happen, maybe Jakka will help him, maybe nothing will happen at all. Yet already a burden is relieved, he feels its absence as he walks that green path, the happy path, the golden path, hunting for those new craftables—runelike fossil fragments, a hidden flowerbed with petals that shed light, a ziggurat of Solo cups that each hold a bonus building tool or tip, are there more, did he find them all?—all the way to the quincunx, where Mathias is not waiting but a message bug is, fat yellow beetle flying in circles, to land on his arm and unfold into SRY CANARY, MEETING, he is glad not to have to talk to Mathias right now.

He still must meet with Clara—heading down the stairs, his step loose and quicker than normal, the relief has followed him into this world too—Clara in her office with a pile of what looks to be brand-new B of P merch, tropical greens and flaring whites, and a man he does not know, bristly blue hair and a BIG DEAD GAMES t-shirt, and "Max," Clara says, "this is Simon. Simon and I worked together at JoJoJo, we're grabbing a catch-up."

"Clara says you're the guru here," Simon rising from the silver swivel chair to extend a hand, big hand, blue skull tattooed halfway up his wrist. "You're sure working that monitor tan, mate," meant to be a friendly joke, but "Max," Clara says, "it's cool, we can run those notes later," her message arriving as he climbs back upstairs, a frowning face then a smiling sun, *U look way tired? Grab some rest.*

Just a headache, Davide used to call it rapture of the deep, that feeling of cranial pressure, will that cease when he becomes Jakka's betanaut? And should he tell Clara about any of that, or what Davide said to her, at her? No, and no: Davide's spite has no bearing on the game itself, and whatever happens, if anything happens, will happen to him alone. And the tasks Clara asks of him—few enough as it is, *the guru here*, more like a figurehead for the digital fleet—he can still accomplish just as well, maybe even better, from inside.

In his room, he pulls the blackout drapes halfway open, swivels his own chair toward the window's sunless light and silvery lines of clouds, leans back to watch that slowly changing sky—then startled upright and awake by the meeting alarm, twenty minutes: to piss, to smile when he sees himself in the mirror, tired, yes, like Lazarus fresh from the cave, but a wash helps, a quick shave and a fresh shirt, a long drink of distilled water, he even considers Ari's old coffee machine still boxed in the corner, the cups are there too—

—as he places the horned mask on the edge of the worktable, who better to explicate a labyrinth than its most famous resident? and "Hey," Ari on-screen and bemused, "it's still there," Ari who looks more like himself than he ever has, shorter hair and winking black earrings, Ari who seems to glow beside a pair of sunstruck windows canted open to the street noise outside, a pair of sirens, a passing blare of music, *Love me baby like a rose rose rose!* "It all looks the same. Except you . . . How come you didn't want to meet in the game, take a walk with me?"

And how to answer that? when a part of him wants that walk, wants it with a sudden plunging pang, Ari the one who understands as no one else can, what would Ari say if he told about Jakka? Instead he retreats into "The maze research, the notes, you got my notes?" and when Ari nods, "I kept it as concise as I could. The key point of the labyrinth is, you're lost until you're not, and then you make your way back out again, if you can. The Minotaur," one hand on the mask, "couldn't."

"Why not?"

"Because Theseus killed him. In the center of the maze," and Ari's face changes, Ari is shocked, no not shocked, a shock confirmed, why? But Ari says nothing, so he goes on: "Ontologically it's about patterns, the power of repeated patterns. Do you remember when we climbed the ramp at the Factory, the night Felix played?"

"And you went up to the roof to look for Jonas."

"Around to go up and around to go down," and around and

around through this world's war of surface and allegory, beside this man on the screen, his friend, best friend, last friend, watching as Ari lights and draws on a cigar, the smoke twisting and curling out the window, Ari who already knows the answers to his questions, the way Shiva knows, the one who makes happen what longs and breathes to happen, friend to the void that swallows or exalts, Ari who never learned about little god Krishna with the mouthful of stars because he already knew that too. "You know the difference between xronos and kairos?"

"You know I don't."

"Xronos means linear time. Kairos means the, the propitious time, the right time—"

"So they could be the same time?"

"You heard Dark Factory's a hotel now? Nothing stays the same," not the Factory, not Mila, not Marfa, not this room, not even the game, nothing is the way it was before or ever will be, proximity to reality always has a cost. "And nothing ever edits out the pain."

"You still want that pain . . . You still down to be my best man?" Ari's smile returning, Ari will always be able to smile. "This time it's a church thing. We're wearing suits, can't wait to see you in a suit. In a *tux*—"

"I can give you my blessing right now," reaching on impulse for the mask, he starts to put it on, the dim weight of it, the smell like room dust and faraway smoke but "No," Ari as suddenly, commandingly, "no, don't," so he stops, holds that empty face a moment, sets it back down, then "You don't need it," he says, "anyway, a blessing."

And now their talk is over, though Ari is saying something about a filmmaker, a documentary, "You should be in it, 'reality artist Max Caspar,' you could school everybody. Sergey's been in the game before, he could do it there . . . What's going on in there, anyway? Bergeron keeps telling Felix it's launching—"

"Tell Felix I said hello."

"I will. Tell Marfa, actually don't tell Marfa—"

"I don't see Marfa anymore. But you should talk to her. No," when Ari rolls his eyes, "Ari, you should. She's the one who knows what this story's all about," as from Ari's window more sirens cry, the empire of the senses calling, for what? to be led out of the maze? or deeper in? Whatever Ari says next he cannot hear, and as Ari rises to close that window, he abruptly disconnects, closes his own window, those drapes that bring the darkness and "Dum vivimus," he says, "vivamus," to the shrieking cat on his arm, the beating heart held high to the sky, he swallows more distilled water, locks the door and logs back in.

TOUCH THE SKY DOC production notes/personal

Always swore I'd never shoot anybody's wedding, but this is Regon and Minos. And Ava Perez the mom, and the pastor (name?), in one of those old urban churches that look airlifted in from the 18th century, light's tricky but great, stained-glass windows and candles. They're wearing suits, dark blue and black, and way over the top pink lily boutonnieres, Regon's legit surprised when Minos pulls out a ring, Minos's mom is like Yes, finally! Minos's mom calls them "Pio" and "Ri."

I'm the other legal witness so my name's on their marriage certificate, that feels wild to me. Regon says, You can put this in your doc, but Minos is clearly not down with that, so I say, This footage is my wedding present to you both, you can do whatever you want with it. While Minos and his mom are figuring out the champagne brunch thing, I say to Regon, You got me here, it changed my life, I'm feeling pretty emotional to be honest, we shake hands. Then I say, Whatever Minos does next, that's going to end the doc. You good with that?

Regon says, Wouldn't want it any different. But call him Felix, that's his name. Then he shows me a photo of Minos, Felix, climbing out of a pool, this really incredible portrait shot, you can <u>see</u> who he is even if you have no clue who he is. I say,

Wow that almost looks like a DeFebvre, and Regon says, Yeah
Miriam sent this to me, never showed it to anyone else before.
Miriam DeFebvre! holy fuck.

***

Tom Hae's MePage features a quote—*God grant me the grace to climb out of my own asshole & see the sky*—Tom Hae calls it "My serenity prayer," Tom Hae in a white collarless shirt, lifting a white teacup to the screen, an open window behind him like a frame around a fairytale, blue sky, pine trees, a gray stone castle; his MePage AWAY message says *Tom Hae is recovering from a jitterbug accident*, whatever that means, but he answered within an hour of Ari's ping. According to the Insomnious bio page, Tom Hae has a master's from Yale Divinity School; on their main page there is only one coded reference to MinosLAB, a graphic of a black sun's rays over a golden mountain, *Transcendence Is Coming*. "Serenity isn't easy to achieve, but I do try . . . You wanted to meet? Without Jason?"

Ari lifts his own drink, black coffee in a paper cup from Café Comida, the apartment quiet around him; Felix is out shopping with Ava, *she wants to buy us towels*. "I did. I do."

"Is Mr. Perez—dissatisfied, in some way, with Jason? I can assure him, and you, that Jason is completely simpatico with MinosLAB's vision. And Jason is a superb technician, his metrics for the platform are—"

"He got canned and banned from Nonstop Studios, legal had to get involved. Why's that?"

Tom Hae sets down his cup. "That isn't public knowledge."

"No it's not."

"I won't ask how you know this. And I won't deny it. Jason had lost his way, existentially, and acted outside of his own best interests. Finding Mr. Perez was key for him. And then of course he introduced me to Mr. Perez's music—You understand, all of this is in strict confidence."

"Sure," and it confirms what he learned from Bergeron and what he knew already, Jase's personal-jesus obsession with Felix, Jase who,

Felix says, has not replied since *I told him I changed my handle,* from Mister Minos to FRegon, *your husband,* Jase sits jealous in the heart of that maze; and Tom Hae is using him to build it. "What did you think of the clip I sent?"

"It's astonishingly raw, Sergey Kendricks is talented. And it's your immense talent, to attract people like Kendricks. And Mr. Perez. And Jason too, in a sense. A hazardous talent, at times."

"Shit can happen," agreeing, shifting in the chair to make sure his screen screens the sofa where Sergey sits filming, Sergey as still as his camera, one calm, focused, documenting eye. "That's why we have to be careful."

"I can assure you, and Jason has repeatedly assured Mr. Perez, that we understand those concerns. Mr. Perez will be completely secure when MinosLAB is launched—"

"MinosLAB can't happen on your platform."

Tom Hae is silent. The wind in that room stirs the curtains, are they real curtains? is it a real room? Then "It's my understanding that Mr. Perez is very eager for this event. If there are issues with the physical host, we can certainly help to address—"

"Not happening on-site, either. Not happening at all."

The wind blows, the curtains move. "Does Mr. Bergeron know this?"

"I'm telling you," Tom Hae presumably the coolest head on this three-headed stack—Bergeron at least is suspicious of Jase, yet Bergeron has his own ongoing jones for Mister Minos, for the chaos he can summon, *what a clusterfuck*—Tom Hae's stare now a money stare, Tom Hae says, "A verbal agreement exists between A Walk in the Park and Insomnious. An enforceable agreement."

"Sure. You can sue us, you have lawyers. We have lawyers too. But that's not going to make anything happen, is it."

"More than a few companies would decline to allow you anywhere near their brands. For a person in that situation, you seem very—confident."

I do try: but no need to say that, to score points or spar anymore, this is not a battle but an annexation, an invitation to "Let go of MinosLAB, and be part of what we're going to do. Felix and me."

"And what is that?"

"It's not what, it's why. Watch that clip again," watching closely but with, yes, serenity, he is sure again of his footing, safe again in thinnest air; and Tom Hae's stare slowly moderates, until "You understand," Tom Hae says, "I find Mr. Perez's work profoundly compelling, personally compelling. When I replay his streams, I hear God—not an entity, you understand. I went to Yale to hear God . . . You're absolutely firm on this?" and when Ari nods, "Then a new discussion's in order. I'll speak to Jason, I'll be in contact with you."

"I'm ready to talk again whenever you are . . . So," with a smile, a change in tone, a sip of his coffee, "what's a jitterbug accident?"

Tom Hae smiles too, a half-smile, showing slightly crooked teeth. "My girlfriend and I were dancing at Lecker, and I lost my footing."

"What's Lecker?"

"A sex club in Wroclaw. Give my best to Mr. Perez."

And as the call ends, Sergey hits pause, stands to stretch, to wince and rotate his shoulder, and "We can't use any of that," Sergey says, "unless he signs a release, zero chance. But you were smooth as glass."

He thinks of Jonas, of Skelly, of Ines. "Not my first time."

"So will they sue?"

"We'll see. I don't think they'll need to, to get what they want. Or at least what he wants."

"Sending that cherrypicker pan was hardcore, surprised a guy like that would like it."

"He didn't say he liked it. He said you were talented—"

—and Sergey laughs, then quickly repositions himself, camera pointing to the door as voices rise on the stairs, Felix and Ava with bags from BUY BUY, thick striped towels and blueberry-blue sheets and "You tell Jai," Ava says, "he owes you a new mattress. A whole new *bed*—"

"Jairo's a clown, we're just lucky there's no bedbugs. Anyway we'll have a new bed soon enough—"

—in their new apartment, part of the plans they have made together, up late last night again, talking, deciding, Felix drinking Bushmills and tap water from a giveaway mug, Ari rising to examine the wooden wall shelves full of left-behind mementos, raveled scarves and clipped wristbands, a JAMAICA OK! ball cap, a red glass jar with a haloed woman playing a piano, *What's this?*

A saint's candle, St. Cecilia. Mrs. G. gave it to me, I never could throw it away . . . Meghan told the church I'm not playing there?

I got hold of the monsignor guy, who seemed primarily annoyed to lose the transaction, the monsignor did not seem to understand who Felix is or what he wanted to do, better that way. *They get to keep the first deposit, so he was fine with it.*

The Bergeron thing was a lot easier than I expected, Felix finally answering all those messages, telling Bergeron that his own trajectory has changed, that Mister Minos is gone, the horned man is a man now, the show is not a game. *I didn't talk to him about Insomnious, though . . . What's going to happen with them? Jase told me his whole life is sunk into this. Jase says the world is a burning candle and MinosLAB is the flame—*

Don't worry. I'll talk to the partner, we'll work it out.

Not to Jase?

No, recalling another Quest Fest clip, the VIP trailer, useless security and claustrophobic crowd, his own blank bewildered face, and Jase murmuring to Felix, mouth close as a kiss to his ear; once Felix had sent him a story about the Minotaur, he still has it, the bull under the bloody star, what had Max said, *you make your way back out again, if you can.* So *No,* he says again. *Not to Jase.*

And Felix half-frowned, not at him, and *You don't like Jase at all,* he said, *do you,* as Ari slowly shook his head.

Now Ava has gone, and Sergey is leaving—"Can't sleep on PT today, I need that range of motion—" so "Come on," Ari says to Felix, tossing him the ASTER BAR ball cap, taking JAMAICA OK! for himself. "Let's go out, you can school me about New York. There's no Kaffee Karts here, a train is a train, and a bodega's a

Späti," but Felix shakes his head, "No, a bodega always has a cat, and *wegbeir*'s not a thing here—"

—as they exit into a breeze that smells like something pleasantly burning, to merge into the sidewalk traffic of backpack toters and noisy teenage wigheads, red streetside trash bins blinking *full full,* a shuttered gym, a gated garden, SIGGY'S SWEETZ and BLUE MOON ASTROLOGY, another block and another in this huge patchwork city that is really many little cities, this mazey place where they will stay, not forever but for a while, *in New York I know a lot of people, we could really make things happen:* some of those things Ari can already sense and see, so much more he cannot, *a hazardous talent,* is that true? does it have to be?

—as a trio of young men abruptly pace them then block them, studded JacBody jackets and oversized green and black caps and "You," says the middle of the three, the leader, pointing at Felix while his friends hold out their phones. "You that DJ played those big messed-up dance shows? Revival-type shows, people talking in the tongues and shit?"

Felix's stance shifts, his shoulders square up. "That's right. I played some shows."

"But you from here?"

"That's right," Felix naming a street, an avenue that Ari does not recognize but the young men do, Ari remembering that desperate boy outside Ava's, what had that boy tried so hard to stick into his pocket? what unseen gift, rejected? so "You like to go to dance shows?" he asks this young man. "You like to dance?"

The young man nods, suddenly cocky and pleased, while his flanking friends laugh, turn their phones on him: "Juan is blast, man. Blast fucking dancer!"

"If you're on Pyramid," Ari's own smile, pointing his own phone, "send me a clip sometime. I'm AriR#1—"

—a clip that arrives as they settle onto a pocket park bench with their takeaway cafecitos: Juan in black workout shorts dancing in a cluttered bedroom to "Off the Cuff," Julian Zero's newest effort, Juan as accomplished a dancer as Julian is a DJ but "He's into it,"

Ari says, showing Felix who shakes his head: "You know that could have easily gone the other way."

"Maybe we should invite him to the show," uncapping his drink to cool it, feeling the sun against his cheek as Felix slips on new sunglasses, his wedding gift, vintage aviator gold, while a couple, pink sun hat and self-consciously grungy beard, kiss against the metal park gate, its black slats hung top to bottom with gaudy rubber love locks. And Felix leans to tap the ring on his finger, pinky finger—"We need to get that sized, baby—" the bronze and beveled wedding band, Felix guessing at his size to keep the surprise but "I like it how it is," he says, and he does, the way it looks and feels, the unaccustomed joy of its existence, *ink is more permanent than rings* but this ring will never leave his finger, this ring proves that love is permanent in his world.

—

And another ring on another finger, Max's ouroboros ring tapping, tapping on the edge of Clara's desk, while Clara frowns and highlights a checkered series of points on her screen, red points, red for warning and "See," Clara says, "here's another bunch. But if it's a user breach, what's it for, ransom? Nobody's hit us up. During Bergeron's stream there was that Solve for X fuckery, but those people are all way gone. Except Davide—"

"You think it's him?" asks blue-haired Simon, Simon sitting on Clara's side of the desk now, but Clara shakes her head: "He's too invested in that woman he follows around, and she works for Leon Cardenal. Max, what do you see here?"

Noting his own nervous tapping, he stops, stares at those blips: Jakka is part of Solve for X, but why would Jakka want to harm a game he seeks to enlarge? Jakka is inside the game now but without an avatar, only a voice, low, busy, dry on the edge of the water, whispering in the forest of no names, asking him oddly basic questions, giving him inconsequential errands to perform that Jakka says are germane to his transformation, Jakka has investigated his profile build too. But whenever he questions Jakka about the continuing delay, *Davide said you already had a workaround?* he gets reams of research denser than Davide's and so convoluted he cannot parse or follow it, and Jakka's assurances, *Pretty quick now Max, pretty quick—*

"Max?"

Too loud, "I'm not seeing anything," technically true but truly a lie, it feels strange to conceal what he knows, but what *does* he know? nothing that would harm the game, and the rest is truly his own business. "But that—anomaly's not causing any problems, is it?"

This time Simon answers, highlighting in yellow a different series of points, *the power of repeated patterns,* Simon looking at him without knowing what he sees: "Well that's what we're trying to figure out, isn't it. And we will figure it out," his staunch lieutenant's nod to Clara who nods back, Clara who has had no one at her side since Meghan Sorin decamped, since Davide was ousted—

—Clara who rises now, one hand on Max's shoulder, to propel him gently out into the hallway, a new prelaunch poster tacked to the Fantastic Fantoms door, WELCOME TO PARADISE and "You won't like this," Clara says, "but Forensics needs a 24-hour logout for all non-essentials. Not that you're not essential, I know this is your baby too. But—"

Lie low, Max, but he now needs to stay in the game, what if those hours are somehow his own long-delayed launch window? will Jakka try him twice? But what else to do except nod, nod and say "It's OK, I'll go do it right now—"

—his own screen glowing a steady tranquil green, a bird of paradise flying forever toward open water, and "OK," he says again, then logs out, watching that bird fade on the wing into a blurry blue background, setting the lockout timer so a corner countdown clock begins, **24:00:00,** now what? He needs to tell Jakka he is temporarily gone, but how to do that outside the game? Davide would know, if Davide would deign to tell him, but none of the several Davide numbers on his phone are viable anymore, and Davide, like him, has no MePage. Would Sheridan know how to reach Davide? Marfa could contact Sheridan, through Leon Cardenal or on her own, yet how should he frame that request to Marfa, how can he ask—

—as on his phone a new message from Ari, unnerving in its strange relevance, *im talking 2 marfa*, as if Ari has been here talking to him, is Ari finally taking his advice about the interview? And could this be the way to approach Marfa? ask about Ari, then ask about Sheridan—

—but the switchback slipperiness of it all, half-truths that are more than half lies, brings a rush of self-disgust so intense that he drops the phone on the table, beside the horned mask still unmoved since his last talk with Ari, *what's going on in there anyway, how come you didn't want to meet in the game, take a walk with me?* his non-answers then just more evasions, evading his friend, evading Clara, is this what he is now, is this his final form? A liar?

He rubs his forehead, another headache unnoticed until now, the game screens out so much. Then out of the chair as if propelled by that disgust, past the knee-high tower of grocery delivery trays, the air mattress baggy with an unknown leak, to grab up his jacket, shove the phone to his pocket, "OK," again and aloud, to who? himself? the mask? "OK, let's take a walk—"

—in this late morning's strange rain, not so much falling as suspended and omnipresent, as if he walks underwater the way he does in the game. But now his hair goes unpleasantly damp, he breathes that dampness in, the sour taste of the street, wet concrete and some ancient vegetal odor, garbage or crushed sidewalk leaves; trucks pass him, trikes pass him, bikes pass him, other walkers pass him, this street has changed from depopulated light industrial to residential lofts and chain cafés and places to buy tech trinkets, when he first used to ride his bike here there was almost no one, he used to ride his bike everywhere . . . Once this world was Y for him, Ari said that, opened in a new and frightening way, a way he meant to explore and understand, but will not, will never: he has become opaque, is almost not here at all, the game is his refuge, the only place left, WELCOME TO PARADISE, yet now he is locked out of there too—

—and half-lost and weary in a district he does not recognize, linden trees and fitness shops and juice bars, a longer walk in this world than he has taken for how long? months? stopping to catch his breath on a sheltered bench outside a brick townhouse building, a dry cleaner on the ground floor, 2 HRS IN & OUT. A young woman already seated there takes one look at him then slides to the bench's very end, a reaction that saddens him. So to seem harmless, like every other person, he takes out his phone and looks at it, looks again at Ari's message, a fleeting half-smile—Ari and Marfa, what a conversation *that* will be—then sees again Ari's video that he never watched, he taps it open—

—on a spiral of shining violence, a body spinning and whipping a glittering flag, more bodies pushing and punching under a maelstrom sky of black and neon green: he and Davide once sat riveted by Felix playing in that silver club, Davide's crow, *That is a soundtrack!* but over these dancers pounds a terrifying, dominating beat, how can human bodies persist at a velocity like that? And what if—a new thought—what if his own human body, his aching head, fails to tolerate whatever strictures Jakka plans to place on it? *Full disclosure, it's buggy, what happened to the first one*—And what if those bugs, those datapoints and whispers, should somehow wing beyond his own avatar? *I'm doing this for Jakka, not for you,* does Davide know more about Jakka's plans than he will say? If Davide hates Clara does Davide hate him too, grudge him that beach and those birds, *keep some of that for yourself, pilgrim*—

—as *You OK?* a message incoming from Marfa, flagged as **URGENT**, *Ari says you went dark on him, what's going on?*

Watching that clip again, its thundering raw desperation, its warning as loud as a sudden scream, he messages *Trying to fix something*—because he needs to talk to Clara now, tell Clara, should he message her? no, this needs to be said face-to-face. Scanning anxious for a Hopper, off the bench and staring down the street as if he could by vision will the car to arrive, tapping his ring in a jittering rhythm on the backseat armrest as that car brakes and crawls through suddenly balky traffic, a real-world collision of matter and velocity, two trucks half-smashed into one ruin, spilling their boxy guts—

—and finally arriving, car to curb to lobby to stairs, breathing hard, heart pounding, head pounding from more than just the exertion—Will Clara be angry, be furious? Will she feel betrayed again, *your baby too,* will she eject him from the game?—up to Clara's office where he does not take time to knock or think or steel himself, only yanks open that door on Clara and Simon still at the desk, eating takeout that smells like hot cow cheese, and "I did it," he says, breathless. "I did it, it's my fault."

"Did what?" Simon half-rising, Clara's gaze startled, then shocked, then guarded and hard as he tells her as quickly as he can everything he knows, and when there is no more to tell, nothing more to say, he says, "I'm fucking sorry, I should have told you before. I never thought—"

"Never *thought*?" Simon incredulous. "How could you not? How could you not even—And this close to launch!"

"I'm sorry," not to Simon but to Clara who now will not even look in his direction, Clara staring pointedly at the door as if she cannot bear the sight of him, but "Go through it," Simon says, pushing a chair his way, "one more time. For Forensics—"

—two new sidebar faces appearing on Clara's screen, two women from Bergeron's forensics team listening as he tells once more his appalling story, feeling the sickness of shame, the fear rising like a fever, his voice never wavers, he tells it all until "Appreciate your, uh, input," one of the women says, black tiara and round pink glasses. "Clara, switching to codecom now," no one looking at him any longer, he is done, dismissed, he leaves the chair, he leaves the room—

—but "Max," Clara sharp to call him back. "Didn't you log out?"

"Before, when you told me to. And set the timer."

"Look," pointing to a figure, his own figure, his own lean avatar scrambling down the dunes, moving in a way he never moves or ever would, almost sly yet strangely bold. "Profile's yours, stats, password, everything. It's you."

"No—no it's him, it's Jakka," Jakka logging in as Max who is almost never logged out, Jakka must have been watching, waiting for a chance, to do what, wreak what ruin in this paradise? so "Delete it," he says, staring over Clara's shoulder at that walking lie, that moving danger. "Delete my whole account. Now."

"Deleting the account," Simon warns, "that'll wipe all your history, that—"

"Deleting your account," says the second sidebar face, black tiara, black corona of hair, "could plausibly be interpreted as an attempt to destroy relevant security data. A self-defensive action—"

"Delete it," again and beseeching, to Clara alone, headache worsening, pounding like his heart, he squints against the pain. "Clara, *please.*"

Clara's mouth turns down at one corner, her gaze never leaves the screen. "Go upstairs, Max. If we need you, we'll message."

So gone again, the stairs an empty mountain, climbing to do nothing but wait, stare out the window as the rain lessens to a glimmer, a scrim, as the countdown clock on his own screen ticks on to a time that is, is it? kairos time? so he writes a message to Ari, a very long message, one long note to annotate what is happening: this doubled identity, this looming death, not his death but in a way it truly and terribly is, *human identity is intrinsically fragile* and this game has shaped his life, been his future, what other future does he have? the pain still rising in his head as he sends that message, his eyes are watering now, he waits for Ari to respond—

—but the response when it comes is from Clara, a one-word message just as the countdown timer freezes on his screen, the green goes bright and solid then gray and flat, white letters, *INVALID USER ID*, Clara's message is *Done* and his game is over.

TOUCH THE SKY DOC production notes/personal

Shooting at HoH should be no problem, just a couple pillars to work around, coordinating with Bon Bon who's running lights night-of, Bon Bon's playing around with spots and projections at walk-thru. Unicorn16's on site this time, they're local, cool to meet in real life, they don't look anything like I expected! I asked, So how'd you get with these guys? and they say, Pure luck, do you believe in luck? Met Marc Blasey too, Blasey used to book for Felix back in the day, and Gus Burns is coming in to record the set for Indigo, Phadrea's working the floor, so it's all fam, super tight. Whole vibe is the total opposite of QF, Regon's making jokes, telling Unicorn16 he can't get good coffee in New York—that espresso company did a limited run brew that's like 300% caffeine and put antlers on the can, Regon says, That can's a collectible now. And Fux is opening, Regon's like why didn't you tell us before that Fuxury is your friend? Fux messaged me, all caps excited, CANT FUCKING BELIEVE IT B2B WITH MINOS!!! THX BRO!!! I tell Fux, You made it all happen.

Biggest issue is security. The show's still hush-hush, it's up as TBA on HoH's New Voices line-up, but what happens when somebody talks? because somebody always talks, are people going to swarm or protest or what? The staff is like, No static, we can handle it. I'm shooting B-roll while they're gossiping about a new DJ feud, one club's infiltrating staff at another club so they can plug in their own players and have staff already on their side, I ask is HoH part of that? and they say, No, this is online, the Y clubs, super cutthroat. But don't shoot this, they'll never let us back in!

Regon's so not worried about security or blowback that I have to ask, What does Meghan say, is Meghan cool with it? Regon gives me this look, he says, Meg says she won't be here. I tell him she said that to me too, but I keep asking her anyway, she has to be here, it's the end of the doc. Told her I'll have a bottle of Cîroc ready for us.

After walk-thru I hit the smoking patio, Regon's out there so I give him a Marlboro Gold, I tell him how that one Marlboro Gold started me up again. He says, Quest Fest changed a lot of things. I ask again about security, but I really mean all of it and he knows I mean all of it, he says, We're in a different place now, tutto bene, am I saying that right?

Back inside, Felix is at the house keyboard, he starts playing a straight classical piece (Bach?), Bon Bon throws a spot on him and everybody goes quiet. When he gets to the last note he bows his head, total silence, you can hear the air blowers kick on. Then Regon starts clapping, everybody starts clapping and whistling, and Felix looks up and smiles, like the smile is part of the music. Of everything I shot so far of Felix, that might be the best thing I got.

***

The night is clear and very mild, and Ari stands alone on the smoking patio with a Riki Taki cigar, one black bootheel tapping to Fuxury's sinewy beats, looking up past the city's low hectic sheen to the stars. He has just scanned again through Max's incredibly long message about having to leave the B of P world, about transhumanism, paracosm, para-reality, nonbeing, all of it so incredibly unhappy and so earnestly, touchingly Max that when Marfa had messaged again, *What the fuck's going on with Max!?* his answer was *hes fine*—because Max *is* fine, Max only needed to get back to being fully Max, start doing what he told Max to do when he first read that message, exactly what Felix is doing tonight: *ok now just go play*

The patio door swings open, Rocky the barback—"We didn't have any peppercorns, so we used hot sauce. Hope that's all right?"—Rocky offering a double hotgrass shot, watching as he throws back that shot, sucks in a big breath, lets it out in a whoosh and a laugh and "It's perfect," he says. "Keep you alive forever." And he smiles at Rocky who smiles back, Rocky has one broken front tooth, Rocky guards his smiles so this one is a gift, and "You ready," he asks Rocky, "for tonight?"

"Yeah, I hope so—I mean, it's wild," with a kind of nervous pleasure, Rocky has clearly heard a lot about the former Mister Minos, and the house is jammed: once the secrecy of the TBA imploded—who told, and does it matter—the tickets disappeared and the posting blew up, *Says FRegon but its Mister Minos! Thought Minos was sued & couldn't play?? FUCK THAT DUDE, o i cant wait, Wouldnt go if it was free, Gracias House of Hello!!!!* and within the hour Beat Buzzer and Tickets Please had pre-review editorial links up, pro or con who knows, and does that matter either. Ilias and Gussie are already set up to record, Bergeron is present via link, joined by Tom Hae dressed all in white like a cosmopolitan vampire, though Jase is not with them, not streaming at all; Upsetta is here, and Clarence Kiz, and Julian Zero—Julian back to being a bushy blond, Julian whose hug was immediate and lingering, Julian who said *Ari god you look great*—and the locals too, Blaze and his crew, Ava of course in a new black sequin blazer, Jairo the slouchy cousin and Jenni the old school friend, even Juan the bedroom dancer and his sidekicks, while Raimundo Silva covers it for Culture Bodega—

—and Meg is here too, Meg whom he feared might not come at all, Meg who deserved so much better from him, who carried all the burdens he abandoned. Meg had not responded to his invitation, but arrived wearing the orchid boutonniere he sent to the B&B—Uni told him she was there, Uni had booked it, Uni recommended the florist too—a lush olive green orchid with a slim pink edge like a smile, a tiny fan of lily grass behind, when Meg messaged *on my way* he messaged back *u like the flower*

Cymbidium. It's my favorite

i know ♥ im sorry miss u so much

♥

—Meg who has her own guest in tow, Suze the sculptor in a severe double-breasted ivory suit, Suze now apparently deep in collaboration with Meg; Sergey is involved somehow too, he will have to ask Sergey about all that. But not tonight, tonight Sergey is the busiest person in the club, has been here for hours and will stay, Sergey says, *Until we're done—*

—Sergey entering the patio now, following Felix and Uni's conversation "—Landlord's cool with it if you are," Uni nodding to Ari to include him in that talk. "It's not huge-huge, but it's big. And it's got a Middle Village type of vibe—"

"I don't know what that is," Ari says.

"I do," Felix says. "We'll go look at it tomorrow. Thanks, Uni."

Uni nods, then doubletaps their glowing earbead, listens, and "Phadrea," they say to Ari, "Phadrea says champagne's up," a champagne toast sponsored by Indigo, to welcome Felix back to the decks, and baptize FRegon's first gig: Ilias is beyond excited but

Not gonna push this time, his message to Ari, **just 100% the beats!!!**

"Fuxury's ready with the intro. Tell him two minutes?"

"Tell him five."

As Uni exits, Sergey angles sideways, changing the shot, but Felix steps deliberately off-camera, Felix in a simple black MC Lee jacket, beard gone, curls wild again, Felix smiling yet serious to say to Sergey, "Hey, this film, your film—It's really incredible. Sorry I was such a dick about it sometimes," to bring Sergey's own half-smile, and "Well," Sergey says, the only time Ari has heard him respond while shooting, "you're the talent."

Then Felix turns back into the light, turns to Ari—"You ready?"—because Felix is ready: no more pounding freefall edge or struggle to keep up, his new beats are effortlessly simple, paired with the dart and swoop of the keyboard, and an even more complex underlay of sounds, all the sounds of this last year: the prickling of a lav mic, a plunge tub's splash and an elevator's open-door ting, feedback at sound check and the faraway howl of crowds, Sergey's focusing murmur, *OK looks good good good,* and Meg sounding perplexed, *We need to get down the mountain, how do we get down that mountain?* And a moment of Ari's own rolling laughter, he had laughed again when Felix played it for him and *That,* Felix had said, *that's from when you were talking to my mom, about what to wear to the gig . . . It feels like when I first started to play, I played and they danced* and now "I'm going to open with Orfeo," Felix says, "'Wife of the Song,' remember that? First thing I ever played here, it was the big banger that summer, Genie loved it. And after that, it's beats till whenever—"

"Beats and the keyboard . . . And I'm going to dance tonight," softly, "with everybody. Out on the floor, right?"

"Right," as softly. "All right."

From inside the chant begins, the nightly House of Hello welcome for the headliner—"Hello, hello, hello, hello—" Fuxury's beats rising to meet it, ride it, amplify it, and "OK," Felix says on a breath, a smile. "Here we go—"

"Make me dance—"

—his own smile begun in the heart of the hum, the joy already in his body, because there is no need for the mountaintop, there is nowhere that hum is not, molecular, invincible, alive, *better than alive,* the pleasure and the loss and the pleasure again: in their world and the wider world, its axis broken and realigned, maybe breaking again, Max used to talk about that, *chaos and the void,* and he only needs to check News Immediate or the Globalist to see that Max is right; Felix sends him things too, articles, predictions . . . But there is no need to ever fear a fall, the hum is in the fall too, and the rise again, the big spin, sometimes Felix says *What are you thinking?* and he always smiles back, what had he said to Meg, before? so long before, **ITS A LOT—**

—taking one last draw on his cigar, turning directly to the camera in that halo of smoke and "Hello," he says, "hello again," then holds the door for Felix, for Sergey's light, for the patio lights and the stars.

The room is still dusty, the drapes still open, the mask on the bare desk with its horns and its heft, potency and latency, Max gives it a glance, whose mask is it now? then checks to see if the trash needs emptying, folds the old neck pillow into thirds to stuff it into a bag with the water purifier filters and a black hoodie that might be Ari's, and leaves, leaving the door unlocked behind him.

Downstairs he sits in the kitchen at the cemetery table, a few new stickers there for games he has never heard of, HILLS OF LAST DESTRUCTION, ZALLEYBASHERS; he remembers Simon's t-shirt, BIG DEAD GAMES. Clara said she should be in the office today, though the launch keeps her more than busy: Clara is everywhere, interviews and profiles, sometimes with Mathias, often with Simon—

—who pokes his head past the doorway, startled then stiffly polite—"Didn't know anyone was here. There's some Z Water in the fridge, help yourself—" and "Thanks," his answer as polite, politely reaching for one of those waters as Simon retreats.

He has not been in this place, this building, since that terrible afternoon, the blanked screen, his headache reaching an unbearable crescendo, temporarily erasing his vision, sending him blind and vomiting to the hospital overnight, two nights, that memory is blurred with confusion and fear and drugs that stunned him past the pain into sleep. Then the long string of clinic visits, the doctors' wrangling, an ophthalmologist, a neurologist, and meds with names like rejected game landscapes, Imitrex, Emgality. Perched on exam tables, stretched out in a tilted chair with a chilled and weighted eye mask like a swooning Victorian consumptive, he had time to think—of Marfa in that pub, *Isn't it enough?* and Marfa at Sugar Shack, *you should still be able to live*—until finally he started to laugh, laugh at himself, and his laughter drew someone, a nurse, an aide, he never saw the face but the voice was kind: *It's not easy being in the dark, is it?* Finally the doctors reached a provisional diagnosis, idiopathic migraine related to stress and severe eyestrain, they gave him different pills and a follow-up appointment, he used none of it, the headaches have not returned.

Throughout it all Marfa kept messaging, *Pavel's got a medicinal honey blend, he can bring it by? Clara says you moved out of the office, where you headed? Max what is going ON* until finally he messaged back *I'm fine, tell Pavel thanks, we should meet up.* He misses Marfa far more than he ever thought he could, oddly misses her more than he had ever missed Mila; and to be her friend now means to enter her new life, but that will take some time.

Meanwhile he has moved, into the smallest bedroom in a small flat not too far from Deborah's place, the other two residents are coders; Clara helped him find it, Clara is a far better friend to him than he deserves. Clara has never told him what Jakka intended, and no one in the outer gaming world knows the story, but there are murmurs enough for him to understand that he was a Trojan horse, a Trojan pony, for some manner of stealth data sponge, a black hole meant to fatally alter the game, turn it into what Mathias calls Armageddon Beach . . . Mathias does not speak to him at all anymore, only about him, Mathias calls him Caspar, never Canary. Clara had told him that *Mathias was all for banning you, but I said no. I said no matter what, Max loves this game.*

I do. But Mathias is right.

See, Davide would never have said that! You know that Cardenal woman kicked Davide to the curb? And Forensics got his number when they got Jakka, so if he tries to get in again—snapping her fingers, a sharp guillotine snap, Clara is finally done with Davide.

It was Clara's compromise with Mathias that allowed him back into B of P, permanent restricted usage, Mathias insisted on that, but he does not feel excluded, instead is grateful that no lasting evil came to the game through him, grateful that he is allowed to play at all. And now that the game is live, the birds have become a flock so large that far fewer of them know him or seek him out, he is just a player among the other players, a living player in this living game that he knows with such intimate knowledge, *your baby too,* always. He has a new handle, Zwiebel, and a stock avatar with a blue onion for a head—*everyone believed that the moon was a giant onion,* his own private tribute to Davide, because no matter what grudges or follies Davide truly loves this game too; Davide could not have known, or knowing countenanced, what Jakka meant to do, Davide let his own needs fool him too.

And Davide knew before he did that it was time to teach the skulls to sing, to talk, a new language of terror and peace, a language beyond words there under the leaves, on the dunes, in the waves, with the garbage and the jewels, akin in its own way to that documentary, Ari keeps sending him clips, Ari who saw and said the truest thing of all, **ok now just go play.**

Someday Ari will play this game with him.

Now he finishes the Z water, sets the empty bottle neatly in the small steel sink, sends Clara a message only Clara will understand, to make her smile, **Finally got that golden shower.** Bags in hand, he heads down the stairs to the busy lobby, to a modest new five-speed bike, out to the street lit today with brassy here-and-gone sunlight, wheeling off slowly but gathering speed, *homo ludens,* meat man, power user, *absolute bodhicitta*—

TOUCH THE SKY DOC production notes/personal

Marfa Carpenter is a real-life Modo Maman, tell her no and she just keeps on bulldozing. Told her I've got an NDA and she's like, Yeah pretty sure that doesn't apply to me. Meghan says, Marfa knows a great deal about Dark Factory, you two might want to consider collaborating? Zero zero zero chance!

But Carpenter's talked to everybody, Carpenter says she can hook me up with Vondie Berenson, Berenson shot Factory documentation with Michelle Cosismo before the site got sold—I read that interview, Cosismo said there are other sites, satellite sites, Cosismo said <u>Vondie and I could make a whole doc feature. Or a series.</u> I want to see what else Berenson shot, I bet Berenson sees the sparks too.

Carpenter asks me about *Touch the Sky*, and how Insomnious is funding the trailer to use on their new platform—that's a whole other NDA with Tom Hae, glad to have Regon's lawyers on my side for that one—and how I'm shooting the Maenad short with Meghan and Suze for the gallery show. But what she really wants me to talk about is Regon, she just keeps circling him, she says, So Ari's living in New York, and Felix is teaching some DJ lab residency at Beat Shack? Thought Quest Fest trashed his career but boom, he's back, he's a big deal again, Ari set all that up? I say, Ask him. She says, Ari won't talk to me.

The one thing she never asks about is the footage itself, if she did what would I say? I don't have any answers, I don't know how it will work on that platform, I don't even know how to write the logline for it. I don't even know what it is.

Regon knows. But I don't ask him.

***

Fux got with me really late last night—they sent another remix of the B2B set from HoH, we're using it as the trailer intro—and I thanked them again, I said I'm putting you in the film acknowledgments, Fux says What for? and I say, For saying *Serge look look*.

And thanks to Meghan too, for being who you are, there's no one like you. Thanks Felix, Minos, FRegon, and thanks Regon, especially Regon for watching my film in the first place, for seeing me. Should probably thank Alastair, for *Ace or Deuce*, Alastair I hope your messed-up life turned out OK. And thanks I guess to Max Caspar, for burning down that garage.

***

My great and ongoing thanks to

Christopher Schelling
Charlie Athanas
Diane Cheklich
K.Guillory/Aemeth
Rick Lieder
Maryse Meijer
Aaron Mustamaa
Kevin Peterson
Quinine Hours
Carter Scholz
Mike Thorn

and special thanks to Tricia Reeks, for continuing to
dream along and host this wild party

—Kathe Koja

KATHE KOJA writes novels and short fiction, and creates and produces immersive performances that cross and combine genres. Her work has won awards, and been optioned for film and performance. kathe@darkfactory.club

ARI REGON is a producer who loves dance music and lives a 25-hour day.

MAX CASPAR is a reality artist and game theorist, and part of the development team behind Birds of Paradise.

MARFA CARPENTER is an arts and culture journalist whose ongoing project, *Making It Real: The Dark Factory Interviews*, is the definitive history of the Dark Factory phenomenon. Want to tell your story? Reach her at marfa@darkfactory.club

FELIX PEREZ is a musician.

SERGEY KENDRICKS is a documentary filmmaker and founder of Tutto Bene Productions. His films include *Ace or Deuce, Housefly, Constructive Panic,* and the upcoming *Touch the Sky.* His work has won the Creative Imaging Award, Atlanta Docs' Special Jury Award, the Jugband Award, and the Iris Foundation's Outstanding Documentary award, among others.